THIS ROUGH MAGIC
Stage 5

Corfu is one of the most beautiful of the Greek islands. It is a place of sunshine, poetry, mystery. It is possibly the magic island that William Shakespeare was thinking of – the island where Prospero practises his 'rough magic', in the famous play *The Tempest*.

Corfu is also very close to the unfriendly coast of Albania, which, at the time of this story, was a 'closed' country with no communication or trade with the world outside. It was difficult to get into Albania, and even more difficult to get out. But the islanders of Corfu have always been adventurous people, and small boats could slip in and out at night without being seen.

Lucy Waring wants only to enjoy her holiday in the spring sunshine. She is not interested in mysteries and secret journeys by boat at night – until people begin to be hurt. Then she is too warm-hearted to stand aside, and soon learns that there is a dark side to the magic island where dolphins swim in the clear blue sea.

Mary Stewart (1916–) is a very well-known and popular author, whose novels have been bestsellers in many countries. Several of her books are set in Greece, a country she knows and loves well.

OXFORD BOOKWORMS
Series Editor: Tricia Hedge

OXFORD BOOKWORMS

For a full list of titles in all the Oxford Bookworms series,
please refer to the *Oxford English* catalogue.

～ Black Series ～

Titles available include:

～ Stage 1 (400 headwords)
*The Elephant Man *Tim Vicary*
*The Monkey's Paw *W.W.Jacobs*
Under the Moon *Rowena Akinyemi*
*The Phantom of the Opera *Jennifer Bassett*

～ Stage 2 (700 headwords)
*Sherlock Holmes Short Stories
  Sir Arthur Conan Doyle
*Voodoo Island *Michael Duckworth*
*New Yorkers *O.Henry* (short stories)

～ Stage 3 (1000 headwords)
*Skyjack! *Tim Vicary*
Love Story *Erich Segal*
Tooth and Claw *Saki* (short stories)
Wyatt's Hurricane *Desmond Bagley*

～ Stage 4 (1400 headwords)
*The Hound of the Baskervilles
  Sir Arthur Conan Doyle
*Three Men in a Boat *Jerome K. Jerome*
The Big Sleep *Raymond Chandler*

～ Stage 5 (1800 headwords)
*Ghost Stories *retold by Rosemary Border*
The Dead of Jericho *Colin Dexter*
*Wuthering Heights *Emily Brontë*
I, Robot *Isaac Asimov* (short stories)

～ Stage 6 (2500 headwords)
*Tess of the d'Urbervilles *Thomas Hardy*
Cry Freedom *John Briley*
Meteor *John Wyndham* (short stories)
Deadheads *Reginald Hill*

Many other titles available, both classic and modern.
**Cassettes available for these titles.*

～ Green Series ～

Adaptations of classic and modern stories for younger readers.
Titles available include:

～ Stage 2 (700 headwords)
*Robinson Crusoe *Daniel Defoe*
*Alice's Adventures in Wonderland *Lewis Carroll*
Too Old to Rock and Roll *Jan Mark* (short stories)

～ Stage 3 (1000 headwords)
*The Prisoner of Zenda *Anthony Hope*
*The Secret Garden *Frances Hodgson Burnett*
On the Edge *Gillian Cross*

～ Stage 4 (1400 headwords)
*Treasure Island *Robert Louis Stevenson*
*Gulliver's Travels *Jonathan Swift*
A Tale of Two Cities *Charles Dickens*
The Silver Sword *Ian Serraillier*

OXFORD BOOKWORMS COLLECTION

Fiction by well-known authors, both classic and modern.
Texts are not abridged or simplified in any way. Titles available include:

From the Cradle to the Grave
  (short stories by *Saki, Evelyn Waugh, Roald Dahl,
  Susan Hill, Somerset Maugham, H. E. Bates,
  Frank Sargeson, Raymond Carver*)

Crime Never Pays
  (short stories by *Agatha Christie,
  Graham Greene, Ruth Rendell, Angela Noel,
  Dorothy L. Sayers, Margery Allingham,
  Sir Arthur Conan Doyle, Patricia Highsmith*)

This Rough Magic

Mary Stewart

retold by
Diane Mowat

OXFORD UNIVERSITY PRESS

Oxford University Press
Walton Street, Oxford OX2 6DP

Oxford New York
Athens Auckland Bangkok Bombay
Calcutta Cape Town Dar es Salaam Delhi
Florence Hong Kong Istanbul Karachi
Kuala Lumpur Madras Madrid Melbourne
Mexico City Nairobi Paris Singapore
Taipei Tokyo Toronto

and associated companies in
Berlin Ibadan

OXFORD and OXFORD ENGLISH
are trade marks of Oxford University Press

ISBN 0 19 421665 9

Original edition copyright © Mary Stewart 1964
This simplified edition © Oxford University Press 1991

First published 1991
Fifth impression 1995

Illustrated by Rachel Ross

Typeset by Hope Services (Abingdon) Ltd
Printed in England by Clays Ltd, St Ives plc

1

The magic island

'And if it's a boy,' Phyllida said cheerfully, 'we'll call him Prospero.'

I laughed. 'Poor child! But why Prospero? Oh, of course, because of Prospero in *The Tempest*. Corfu was Shakespeare's magic island in *The Tempest*, wasn't it?'

'Yes. We've already got one character from the play here – Miranda. And her brother's called Spiro, which sounds a bit like Prospero, doesn't it? Miranda and Spiro are twins.'

My sister smiled at me, and reached for the coffee pot. 'More coffee, Lucy?' she asked.

We were having breakfast outside in the sun, on the terrace of my sister's house on the beautiful island of Corfu, which lies off the west coast of Greece. Below the terrace, wooded cliffs fell steeply to a small, sheltered bay, where the sea lay calm and still. From where we sat, we could not see the bay, as it was hidden by the trees. But we had a wonderful view out across the sea, and to the north we could just see the snow-topped mountains of Albania in the distance.

My sister Phyllida is three years older than I am, and when she was twenty she married a Roman banker, Leonardo Forli. The Forli family had owned land on Corfu for many years and Leo's great-grandfather had built an enormous house, the Castello dei Fiori, in the woods above the bay. Later, Leo's father had built two smaller, more modern houses on the cliffs on the north and south sides of the bay. The house on the northern side was called the Villa

Forli, and it was used by Phyllida and Leo. The house on the southern side was called the Villa Rotha, and it stood above the big boat-house which Leo's great-grandfather had built. This villa was rented by an Englishman, Godfrey Manning, who had been there since the previous autumn. He was writing a book, Phyllida had told me, and was taking a lot of photographs for it. The three houses were connected with the main road by the private road up to the Castello, and connected to each other by various paths through the woods and down to the bay.

That spring Phyllida was expecting her third child and the heat in Rome was too much for her. Therefore, Leo had persuaded her to go to Corfu, and to leave the other two children, who were at school, in the care of their grand-mother in Rome. Leo, of course, was working, but he was going to visit Corfu at weekends whenever he could.

Phyllida had asked me to go and stay with her, and her invitation had come just at the right time. I'm an actress and the play I was in, my first in London, had closed after only two months. I was feeling very miserable. It had been a bad winter, and I was tired, depressed, and seriously wondering – at the age of twenty-five – if I should look for a different job. So it was wonderful to find myself on this magic island, with the sun shining brightly. It was far away from the cold of an English April.

I sat back in my chair, drank my coffee, and enjoyed the peace and beauty as I looked out towards the distant snows of Albania.

'Well, Corfu is certainly a magic island for me,' I said dreamily. 'Who are these Shakespearean twins of yours, anyway?'

'Oh, they're Maria's children. Maria's the woman who works for us here. Miranda helps her mother here, and Spiro works for Godfrey Manning at the Villa Rotha. Maria and the twins live in the village.'

But I could see that Phyllida had something else that she wanted to tell me.

'Someone very famous is renting the Castello,' she informed me.

'What? That huge old house?' I said. 'Who wants to rent that?'

'Julian Gale.'

'Julian Gale!' I sat up suddenly and stared at Phyllida in surprise. 'Do you mean Julian Gale, the actor?'

'Yes,' my sister replied, pleased by my excitement.

Julian Gale had been one of Britain's finest actors for many years, and then two years ago, he had suddenly left the theatre and disappeared.

'So he came here,' I said. 'I knew he was ill after that terrible accident, but then he just disappeared.'

'Yes, well,' Phyllida said, 'he doesn't go out and nobody is allowed to go to the house, so I don't imagine that you'll even meet him.'

'*The Tempest* was the last play he did,' I said. 'He was wonderful in it. I remember crying my eyes out over the famous "this rough magic" speech. Is that why he came to Corfu?'

Phyllida laughed. 'I don't think so,' she replied. 'He was here during the war, and then he stayed on afterwards. Before his wife and daughter were killed in the accident, they all used to come here for holidays. He probably just remembered the Castello when he needed to disappear.'

Just then a young girl of about seventeen came in. She was wearing a red dress, which went well with her dark skin and hair. She had come to take away the breakfast things. She looked at me curiously, and then she smiled.

'This is Miranda,' explained Phyllida. 'If you want to go swimming this morning, I'll ask her to show you the way.'

'I'd love to,' I replied.

Phyllida turned to Miranda. 'Will you show my sister the way to the beach when you've finished that, Miranda?'

'Of course,' Miranda said, smiling.

The way to the beach was through the trees, and in a while we came to a fork in the path. The downhill path led to the beach and the uphill one, Miranda told me, was the private path to the Castello.

'Where's the other villa? Mr Manning's?' I asked.

'On the other side of the bay, at the top of the cliff,' she replied. 'You can't see it from the beach because of the trees, but there's a path from the boat-house up the cliff. My brother Spiro works there.'

'What about your father?' I asked her. 'Where does he work?'

'My father left us many years ago. He went over there.' She pointed towards Albania. 'He was a communist. Nobody can travel to Albania, so we don't know if my father is alive or dead.' Her eyes grew bright. 'But we have Spiro,' she said.

'Well, thanks very much, Miranda,' I said. 'Please tell my sister that I'll be back for lunch.'

I turned down the steep path under the trees. At the first bend I looked back. Miranda had gone, but I thought I saw something red on the forbidden path to the Castello.

2

A meeting

The bay was very quiet and there was no one else there. I changed into my swimsuit very quickly, under the trees. Then I crossed the hot, white sand. The blue-green water felt cool and silky and I swam gently along near the shore. Then I turned and floated lazily on my back, with my eyes closed against the bright sun.

Suddenly, I felt something cold swim past my leg. Afraid, I looked around wildly to see what it was. I saw something coming back towards me. 'Sharks!' I screamed silently. I didn't wait, but swam madly towards the rocks. When I reached them, I managed to pull myself up and climb out of the water. Then I turned to look again. It wasn't a shark. It was a dolphin. He lay quietly in the water and looked at me with his bright eyes. I watched him in delight. I knew what he wanted. The dolphin was inviting me, Lucy Waring, to go into the water and play with him.

But as I was about to go back into the water to join him, I heard a strange sound. Something flew past my ear and hit the water in front of the dolphin. It happened again. And suddenly I realized what was happening. These were bullets – someone was shooting at the dolphin. The shots were coming from the woods above the bay, and I shouted as loudly as I could, 'Stop that shooting! Stop it at once!'

I swam forward quickly into the sunlight. I hoped that my

rough movement would frighten the dolphin and that he would swim away from the danger.

It did frighten him. He went under the water and disappeared.

I turned to look up at the cliffs. I could see the top of the Castello dei Fiori and its terrace. There was a man standing there, watching me. It was not Sir Julian because this man was too young and too dark. Perhaps it was his gardener.

I was very angry. Quickly, I picked up my things and ran towards the steps which led up to the terrace. The man waved to me and pointed southwards. 'That way, please,' he shouted in English.

I didn't listen. I was going to tell him what I thought and I went up those steps fast. Suddenly I came face to face with the man. He had come down to meet me and was waiting for me.

'This is private ground,' he said coldly. 'Perhaps you'll be good enough to leave the way you came. This only takes you to the terrace, and then through the house.'

I wasted no words. 'Why were you shooting at that dolphin?' I asked.

He looked surprised and puzzled. 'What are you talking about?' he said.

'Don't pretend that you don't know. I saw you.'

'I certainly saw a dolphin,' he admitted, 'but I didn't see you until you shouted and jumped out from the trees. But you must have made a mistake. I heard nothing. Anyway, why would anybody want to shoot a dolphin?'

'*I'm* asking *you*,' I said.

For a moment I thought I had said too much. He frowned

angrily, and as we stared at each other in silence, I noticed him properly for the first time.

I saw a strongly built man of about thirty, carelessly dressed, with dark hair and eyes. His appearance suggested an aggressive character, I thought, but there was also something sensitive about the mouth. However, at the moment the aggressiveness was much more noticeable.

'Well,' he said sharply, 'I'm afraid you'll have to take my word for it. I did not shoot at the dolphin. And now, please excuse me. Would you please—'

'Go back the way I came? All right. I'm sorry. Perhaps I was wrong about you, but I wasn't wrong about the shooting. If it wasn't you, do you know who it was?'

'No.'

'Not the gardener?'

'No.'

'Or Mr Manning?'

'No. He's been taking photographs of the dolphin for weeks. He and the Greek boy, Spiro, tamed it.'

'Oh. It wouldn't be him, then. Well, we'll just have to try and stop the person who's doing it, won't we?'

He said quickly, 'We?'

'Yes. I'm Lucy Waring, Phyllida Forli's sister. Are you staying with Sir Julian?'

'I'm his son. So you're Miss Waring. I hadn't realized you were here already.' He hesitated. 'Is Leo Forli at home now?'

'No,' I said shortly, and turned to go.

'I'm sorry if I was a little rude,' he apologized. 'We've had so many people here lately, and my father . . . he's been ill and he came here to get better. He needs peace. And I'm a musician. I need quiet to work.'

'Well,' I said, 'I'm sorry if I've stopped you from working. I'll go now and let you get on with it. Goodbye, Mr Gale.'

He left, and soon I heard voices, and then music.

I could be sure that I was already forgotten.

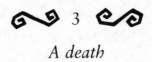

3

A death

When I had taken a shower and dressed, I felt calmer and I was ready to tell Phyllida all about the dolphin and the disagreeable Mr Gale. I went out onto the terrace, but she wasn't there. Miranda and her mother weren't there either.

Then I heard the door from the kitchen open, and my sister came into the living-room.

'Lucy? Is that you?' she called.

'I'm out here,' I replied, and I went towards the french windows, which led into the living-room. One look at her face made me forget everything.

'Phyl! What's the matter? You look terrible!'

'Something awful has happened. Poor Maria's boy has been drowned, Spiro, the boy I told you about at breakfast.'

'Phyl! How terrible! But – how? When?'

'Last night. He was out with Godfrey on the boat – you know, Godfrey Manning – and there was an accident. Spiro fell over the side of the boat and was drowned. Godfrey's come over to tell us, and I've just told Maria and Miranda. I've sent them home now.' She put a hand to her head. 'Lucy, it was so awful! Godfrey's still here. Come and meet him.'

We went through into the living-room. At the far end there was a man with his back to us. He was pouring himself a drink. When we came in, he turned. He was tall and toughly built, with brown hair made lighter by the sun, a narrow, clever face and tired grey eyes. He was probably about thirty-five years of age.

Phyllida introduced us, but he was really more interested in her than in me. 'You've told them?' he said. 'Was it very bad?'

'Worse than bad.'

'Of course. Look, Phyl, do you think I should go and talk to them now?'

'No. Wait. Just at the moment I don't think Maria can believe that Spiro's dead.' Phyllida looked up at him. 'Godfrey,' she said, 'I suppose there's no doubt, is there? He really is dead?'

'Well, that's it, you see. That's why I didn't come here immediately. I've been phoning. I was trying to discover if his body had been found. But I'm sure he can't be alive. I saw him go over the side.'

'What happened?' I asked.

'Do you know,' said Godfrey, 'I'm still not really sure. I'm beginning to wonder just how much I really do remember. I'm sorry.'

'Perhaps you don't want to talk about it. I shouldn't have asked,' I said.

'It's all right. I've already talked to the police and I've told Phyl about it. The worst thing is that I'll have to talk to the boy's mother.' He looked at me directly for the first time. 'You hadn't met Spiro?' he asked.

'I only arrived last night, but Phyl told me about him.'

'I suppose there's no doubt, is there?' said Phyllida.
'Spiro really is dead?'

Godfrey continued, 'I came here last year, and he's worked for me since then. He was a clever mechanic. He knew everything about boats. You know I'm writing a book and I need a lot of photographs for it? Well, Spiro helped me with those, too. In fact, I used him in some of them.' He paused for a moment and then the tired grey eyes came back to me.

'I'd been taking some photographs at night, and I wanted to get some of the sun when it rose over the mountains with the snow still on them. Spiro and I took my boat out last night. There was some wind, but nothing to worry about. The sea wasn't really rough. I was below in the cabin, working on my camera, and suddenly the engine stopped. I went up on deck to see what had happened. Spiro was hanging over the side at the back of the boat. He was trying to find out what was wrong. I think I called to him to be careful, but just then the wind caught the boat and it swung over violently. Spiro was holding the rail, but it was wet and slippery and he lost his hold on it. He tried to catch it again, but missed and went over the side. By the time I reached the back of the boat, I couldn't even see him. He had disappeared.'

'He couldn't swim?' I asked.

'Oh, yes. But it was very dark and the boat was drifting fast. The wind was stronger by then, you see. I shouted again and again, but there was no reply . . . In the end I managed to start the engine, and I searched for Spiro for two hours, but it was no good. I couldn't find him.'

'You did all you could,' said Phyllida sadly.

'Yes, but because I didn't find his body, perhaps his mother will hope that he'll come back. If he got as far as

Albania, she could wait for years to discover what happened.'

'Just as she did with his father,' I added.

He stared at me. 'His father! I forgot that! Poor woman! And it's worse because Spiro wasn't expecting to go out with me last night. I only asked him at the last minute.'

Phyllida looked thoughtful. 'Look, Godfrey,' she said, 'when you go home, you'd better take these photographs with you. It wouldn't be very good for Maria to see them now.'

'Oh, yes. Of course.' He picked them up and, for a moment, he looked unsure of himself. Something made me say, 'Are those the photographs for your book?'

'Yes. Would you like to see them?' he asked.

There were several photographs of Spiro and the dolphin, and a wonderful one of them together. It was so good that I said, 'If I hadn't seen the dolphin myself, I wouldn't believe that this was real.'

Godfrey was interested. 'You say you've seen the dolphin?' he asked.

So I told them both about my morning adventure and about my meeting with Mr Gale's son.

'Max Gale!' Phyllida cried. 'Lucy, you're not trying to tell me that Max Gale was running about in the woods with a gun, are you? Don't be silly!'

'Well, he did say it wasn't him,' I said. 'Anyway, he hadn't got the gun any longer, so I couldn't prove it. But I didn't believe him, and he was very rude.'

'Yes, but it couldn't have been him,' Phyllida said.

'Probably not,' agreed Godfrey.

Phyllida looked at him sharply. 'What is it?' she asked.

'Nothing.'

But Phyllida had understood. Her eyes opened wide and her face changed colour. 'Oh, no! But I suppose it could be . . . But Godfrey, that's awful! If he got a gun . . .'

'Look,' I said strongly, 'if you two are talking about Sir Julian Gale, I've never heard anything so silly! He wouldn't shoot a dolphin. Everybody who worked with him loved him. It's not in his character. He couldn't do it – not unless he was drunk, or had gone mad . . .'

I stopped. There was a silence that could be felt. Then Phyllida turned to me.

'Look, you know that Julian Gale disappeared after he left the theatre? You know about the car accident three or four years ago, when his wife and daughter were killed?'

'Yes, of course. What happened? Was he ill?'

'Yes, he was, I suppose. He had a nervous breakdown. He was in hospital for over a year. They say that he's better now, and he does go out sometimes to visit a few friends, but there's always someone with him.'

I said dully, 'You mean they have to watch him? You're trying to tell me that Julian Gale is . . .' I paused. Why was it so difficult to put it into words?

'Oh, look,' said Phyllida, 'when I met him, he seemed perfectly normal. There's probably nothing wrong. He just wants peace and quiet. And Max Gale wants to be left alone to work – he's writing the music for a film of *The Tempest*. That's probably why young Adoni guards the place.'

'Young who?' I said.

'Adoni, the gardener.'

She turned to Godfrey then and said something about Adoni. He had been a close friend of Spiro. Phyllida added something about Adoni, Miranda and a dowry.

Suddenly Godfrey Manning said, 'I must get back home in case anyone phones with some news. By the way, Phyl, when is Leo coming over?'

'I'm not sure, but certainly for Easter, with the children.'

Godfrey said goodbye and left. Phyllida and I sat in silence until the sound of his car was lost in the distance.

'Come on, then, where's lunch?' I said. 'I'm hungry.'

As I followed Phyllida out of the room, I thought that the Gales probably knew about Spiro by now. I had seen Maria and Miranda when they left the house. They had taken the path that led only to the empty bay – or to the Castello dei Fiori.

 4

Another meeting

Days went by, peaceful, lovely days. Every day I went down to the bay to swim. Sometimes the dolphin came and I never left until he did. I wanted to be sure that nobody shot at him again. I also watched the terrace of the Castello, but there was no more shooting.

There had been no news of Spiro, and Maria and Miranda came back to work the day after his death. They moved about the house sadly and silently. Miranda's eyes were often red from crying, and Maria stayed in the kitchen most of the time.

On the Sunday before Easter I went into Corfu town to watch the procession. This is one of the four times in the year when the body of the island's saint, Saint Spiridion, is brought out of the church and carried through the streets. The people believe that he takes care of the island and those who live there, and they love him very much. Therefore the town was very crowded. Spiro's name was really Spiridion, too, and I wondered if Miranda was there.

As the procession passed near me, there was a moment's silence which was broken suddenly by the sound of a woman crying. I turned round. It was Miranda.

When the procession moved on, the crowd began to leave, and I saw Miranda walk quickly away. I went back towards the place where I had left the car. Just then I saw Miranda again. She was standing with her back to me, but her hands were up to her face, and I thought she was crying.

I hesitated, but a man who had been standing near went and spoke to her. He seemed to be trying to persuade her to go with him, but she shook her head.

I decided to go and speak to her. 'Miranda, it's Miss Lucy. I have the car here. Would you like to come home with me?'

The young man turned round. 'Oh, thank you. That's very kind. You must be Miss Waring?'

He was very handsome, and he looked about nineteen.

'Why, yes,' I said in surprise. And then I realized who this was. 'And you're – Adoni?'

'Yes,' he replied, and he smiled. He had very white teeth and beautiful eyes. In fact, he looked just like a young Greek god.

When we reached the car, he took the keys from me and helped Miranda into the back. Then he came and sat beside me in the front. As we were driving, I asked him quietly, 'Will Miranda and her mother have enough money now that Spiro's gone?'

'They'll be cared for,' he replied confidently. 'I'll marry Miranda. There's no dowry, but that doesn't matter. Spiro was my friend. Of course, Sir Gale may give her a dowry. I don't know. It won't make any difference. I'll take her with or without a dowry. Sir Gale will arrange the marriage.'

'Sir Julian?'

'Yes. He's the twins' godfather. Have you met him yet, Miss Waring?'

'No.'

'You've met Max, though, haven't you?'

'Yes.' I decided to talk about something else. 'Do you ever go out shooting, Adoni?' I asked.

He laughed. 'No, Miss Waring. I didn't shoot at your dolphin. No Greek would do so. Ah, here we are. Thank you very much. I'll take Miranda to her mother. Then I've promised to go to the Castello. Max wants to go out this afternoon. Perhaps I'll see you at the Castello soon?'

'I don't think so,' I replied.

I watched Adoni take the silent Miranda through her mother's door, and I thought that it would be nice to have someone to take care of me like that.

As I drove away, I realized that if Max Gale was going to be out, at least I could have my afternoon swim in peace.

I went down to the bay after tea, when it was not so hot, and afterwards I began to climb slowly up the path to the villa. Suddenly I heard a bird cry out in terror. As I ran up the path, the two parent birds met me, screaming loudly. I rushed forward and I saw a beautiful white cat, which was about to attack a baby bird. I did the only thing possible, and dived onto the cat, took him gently by the body and held him. He tried hard to get free, but he didn't scratch or bite. I picked him up and began to carry him away from the birds. He seemed to like this and he started to purr. But he was very heavy, and finally I had to put him down. He looked up at me and then moved away and disappeared.

I followed him out of the shadow of the trees and found myself in bright sunlight, in the middle of a lovely, wild garden. All around me were roses – sweet-smelling roses of every colour, all in full flower. I stood still in delight. It was a beautiful, magical place. Then I remembered that Leo's grandfather had planted these roses when he lived in the Castello. Without thinking, I stretched out my hand and began to pick some of them. The white cat reappeared and sat on the top of a bank, watching me.

Suddenly I heard a beautiful voice coming from just above me. I'd heard this voice many times before, in dark London theatres. It was Sir Julian Gale.

The rose garden, I now realized in alarm, was at the foot of the terrace of the Castello and Sir Julian was standing there, looking down at me through some bushes. I tried to explain about the cat, but he saw the roses in my arms. 'Ah,' he said, smiling pleasantly, 'you've been stealing my roses, I see.'

'Oh, I never thought . . . I'm terribly sorry,' I said uncomfortably.

'Well, now you must pay a forfeit. You must come up and talk to me,' ordered Sir Julian cheerfully.

I hesitated, but it would have been rude to refuse. Slowly I went up the half-hidden steps and came out onto the terrace.

'Come in, Miss Lucy Waring. You see, I know who you are. And here's my son. But, of course, you've already met.'

'Ah,' said Sir Julian, 'you've been stealing my roses, I see.'

Max Gale was sitting in the shade, at a large table which was covered with papers. He didn't seem very pleased when we disturbed him, but Sir Julian insisted that I must stay for a drink. I asked for an orange juice, and received an unexpected, warm smile from Max Gale.

Sir Julian was not handsome, but he was a fine, big man with thick, grey hair. His eyes were tired, but he behaved quite naturally, except when he took his orange juice from Max. His hand shook quite badly.

Sir Julian and I talked for a long time – about the world of the theatre, the latest stories, and finally about myself. I talked, and he was a sympathetic listener. He seemed to enjoy our conversation, and I didn't notice the shadows of the Castello moving towards us. Suddenly I realized that Max Gale was sitting behind us, listening. I felt that I had to say something to him before I left and I asked him if he had seen the procession that morning. We went on to discuss the possibility that Corfu was Shakespeare's magic island in *The Tempest*. Sir Julian repeated what Phyllida had told me – that Max was writing the music for a film of *The Tempest*.

When at last I rose to leave, Sir Julian begged me to visit him again. He came with me to the edge of the rose garden and pointed to the path through the woods. A few minutes later I heard the sound of a piano. Max Gale was working again.

The woods were dark and quiet, and as I went down the path I was thinking about Sir Julian. Suddenly I saw someone coming up the path from the bay. He was coming straight towards me, breathing heavily. He seemed to be trying not to make a noise. I stepped back behind the trees, and waited.

He was Greek, someone I hadn't seen before, a young
man. He stopped, took out a cigarette, but then decided not
to light it. When he turned to go, I saw his face quite clearly.
There was a look of excitement on it which made me afraid.
Carefully, he continued on his way, up the path to the
Castello.

The wind suddenly blew through the trees, and the air
was cool. I stood quite still until I could no longer hear the
sound of the Greek's footsteps.

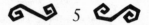 5

The body on the beach

I didn't tell my sister about my visit to the Gales, even
when we passed the path to the Castello on our way to
the bay the next morning.

Before we went into the water, Phyllida took off her ring,
with its huge diamond, and put it into a little plastic beach
bag. Then we went out into the blue-green water to swim. I
looked for the dolphin, but he didn't come into the bay that
day. After a time we went back to the beach, and we lay
there in the sun, talking lazily. Soon Phyllida fell asleep
and I went back into the water. Up on the terrace of the
Castello I could see Sir Julian, and he waved to me. I waved
back, but I was annoyed when I saw someone else watching
me from one of the first-floor windows. Because I was angry
I swam over to the rocks where Max Gale couldn't see me
and came out of the water near the path which led to
Godfrey Manning's villa. Carefully, I made my way along

between the pools until I came to one which was bigger than the others. The dark green water was deep, and the blue-black shadows were alive with the movements of tiny fish. I stared down into the water.

The body was lying half in, half out of the shadow. I hadn't seen it at first because the bright sun was shining straight into my eyes. I felt sick with shock, but, of course, I had to look again. I knelt down, shading my eyes with my hand, and stared into the water.

'Spiro!' I thought, but then the water was disturbed by the wind and the dead man's face moved. I knew him! It wasn't Spiro. It was the man I had seen the night before, the man who was going up to the Castello!

The sunlight was hot on my closed eyes. 'Phyllida!' I thought. 'Phyllida mustn't see this.'

I opened my eyes and hoped that I had been wrong, that there was no dead man. But he was still there.

With difficulty, I got up and made my way over to the rocks near the path to Godfrey Manning's villa. Suddenly I heard a noise. It was the sound of the boat-house door closing. I looked up. Godfrey Manning was coming down the path towards me. 'Lucy! Is something wrong? Are you ill?' he cried.

I couldn't speak. I pointed to the pool. 'Come and sit down,' he said.

I sat down on a rock, with my head in my hands, and then I heard Godfrey go over to the pool.

There was silence for a few moments. I looked up. Godfrey was standing still, looking down. I could see that he was shocked. He, too, must have thought that it would be Spiro.

'Do you know who it is?' I asked.

I thought that he hesitated, but then he replied, 'Yes. His name's Yanni Zoulas. He's from the village.' After a moment he added, 'He was a fisherman, but also a smuggler, I think. He made a lot of trips to Albania. I only hope the police don't find out about that, because I'm afraid that Spiro might have been involved with him in some way.'

'Smuggling!' I stared at him. 'Are you saying this wasn't an accident . . . that you think Yanni Zoulas was murdered?' My voice was rather shaky.

'Good heavens, no!' he replied quickly. 'Nothing like that. It must have been an accident.'

'Has he got a family?' I asked.

'Yes. A wife – they live with his parents. They're going to miss him – and the smuggling. That's how they lived so well . . . Anyway, we'd better go back to my villa and phone the police. Are you all right? Can you move now?'

'Yes, but my clothes are in the bay. Phyl's there, too. She was asleep when I left her.'

I had just finished speaking when Phyllida herself appeared. We tried to pretend that there was nothing wrong because we didn't want to upset her, but Phyllida is not a fool. 'Something's wrong! What is it?' she cried.

'We'd better tell her,' I said to Godfrey. 'She'll find out in the end.'

Godfrey began to explain what had happened. Suddenly he stopped speaking. A shadow fell across me, and then, from behind me, Max Gale's voice said, 'Is anything the matter?'

I jumped. None of us had heard him arrive. He moved like a cat. For a moment nobody replied. Then Godfrey spoke. 'The matter?' he repeated, and all at once I knew that he didn't want to tell Max Gale. I felt cold with fear.

'It's obvious that something's wrong. What is it?' Max Gale insisted.

In the end it was Phyllida who explained.

'Who is it? Do you know?' Gale asked.

'Yanni Zoulas,' I said. 'Did you know him?'

'Why, yes. A little.' All of a sudden his expression changed. 'I wonder what time he went out last night. I thought I heard a boat just after midnight.' He looked thoughtful. 'It must have happened in the last forty-eight hours. I saw his boat myself on Saturday.'

'And', I thought, 'you saw Yanni himself last night, when he came up to the Castello. Why are you saying nothing about that?' But I kept this thought to myself.

'Well, I think we should let the police get on with their job now,' Godfrey Manning said. 'Shall we go? . . . Where are you going?'

Max Gale didn't answer. He was already going down towards the pool where the body lay. Godfrey followed him. They stood looking down at the body. Then Max Gale lay down at the edge of the pool and put his hand into the water.

When they returned, Max Gale said, 'I wonder what the police will think of that. He's obviously been hit on the head quite badly.'

'Well, let's go and call the police, shall we?' said Godfrey.

I still had to get my clothes from the beach. Godfrey offered to go and fetch them, but Max Gale said quickly, 'I'll go and get them and bring them up to the villa.' Clearly, he intended to come and hear what was said to the police, though no one had invited him to go with us.

Godfrey watched him as he went, and his grey eyes seemed strangely cold. Then he saw that I was looking at him. 'Well, this way,' he said.

Phyllida found the climb a little difficult, and Godfrey stopped to help her. I was in front of them and at a corner I turned round to look down at the bay. Through the trees I saw Max Gale down by the rock pool again, lying beside it as before, with his arm in the water. Then he stood up quickly and ran back into the trees. 'So that's why he went back,' I thought.

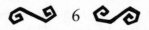 6

Adventure at midnight

Although Phyllida and I spent the rest of the day quietly, she was tired and went to bed early. Maria and Miranda had left after dinner, and the house was very quiet. But I couldn't rest. I kept thinking about everything that had happened.

The police had been. When they arrived at Godfrey's villa, they went straight down to see the body. The last time Yanni's family had seen him was on Sunday, and Max Gale told the police that he had not seen Yanni since Saturday. Yanni's boat had been found. He had had some kind of accident and was dead when he entered the water. The police said nothing about smuggling.

But I was sure that Max Gale was involved in all this.

Perhaps he was the head of the smuggling ring? Nothing was found on Yanni's boat, but perhaps Yanni was on his way back? And Max Gale had probably gone back to the pool to search for anything which could connect him with Yanni. Max Gale had probably shot at the dolphin, too, to keep the tourists away because he needed to be private. But why had I said nothing to the police about seeing Yanni on the path up to the Castello on Sunday night? It was not important, I told myself – but I knew it was.

Just after midnight I heard Phyllida moving about in her room. I went to find out what was wrong. She was very upset and said that she had lost her diamond ring. It belonged to Leo's family and she was very worried about it. We remembered that she had put it in her little bag when we went swimming. She must have left the bag on the beach. She was so upset that I said I would go and fetch it for her.

As I went down the path to the bay, the woods were still and silent. I knew I had no reason to be afraid, but when I came to the place where I had seen Yanni the night before, I suddenly felt cold. From the Castello above I could just hear the sound of Max's piano and the voices of Sir Julian and Max talking.

I continued down the path and left the woods. Quickly I crossed the sand to the place where Phyllida and I had been. Something was lying there! Something long and dark, like a body! For a moment I stood there, frozen with terror. But I had to get the ring for Phyllida. I went nearer. There was no sound, except for the distant piano. Suddenly the shape moved and I saw a living eye watching me. I drew in my breath to scream, but then I saw what it was.

It was the dolphin. Carefully, I went closer. 'What's the

matter? Are you hurt?' I said softly. I shone my torch over him and in the light I saw Phyllida's little bag. I picked it up, put it in my pocket and forgot about it. Just at that moment the dolphin was more important to me. I had to save him. Somehow, he had landed himself on the beach, four metres from the sea. He didn't seem to be hurt, but I had to get him back into the water. I knew that if his skin became too dry, he would die. If somebody didn't shoot him first.

I tried to pull him, but I couldn't. I needed help. Desperately, I emptied Phyllida's little plastic bag and pushed the Forli diamond on my finger. Then I rushed backwards and forwards to the sea, filling the little bag with water and pouring it over the dolphin. At last he seemed wet enough. He would be safe while I went for help. I dropped the wet bag and whispered, 'I'll be back. Don't worry.'

I ran back across the beach. The piano had stopped, but I could see the light from the terrace window. Then I was in the shadow of the woods where the path to the Villa Forli rose steeply. I began to climb up it, but stopped to rest for a moment under a tree. Then I set off again. Ahead of me on the path something moved! I switched on my torch quickly and I saw a man step off the path. The next minute there was a sound beside me and he jumped out at me.

My torch fell from my hand and I was about to scream, but he pulled me to him violently, and his hand came down hard on my mouth.

7

A suspect

He was very strong. I fought hard, but I couldn't do anything, although I must have hurt his hand because he took it away. 'Keep quiet, will you!' he ordered in English, and then he pushed my face hard against the front of his jacket. I stopped fighting, and he loosened his fierce hold on me. I pulled my head free. If I screamed, they would hear me in the Castello. They could be down here in a few seconds . . . surely . . . even Max Gale—

'Where have you been?' demanded the man.

I stared at him. '*You*?' I said.

'Have you been up at the Castello?'

'I have not, and if I had—'

'Then you've been to the beach. Why?'

'I went down to get Phyl's ring, if you must know. She left it on the beach this morning. There! You see?' I held out my hand with the diamond ring on my finger. 'And now, Mr Gale, what exactly do you think you're doing? You hurt me!'

'I'm sorry. I thought you were going to scream.'

'Of course I was. And why shouldn't I? What have you been doing – that's so secret?'

'Fishing.'

'Oh . . . but you were up there at the Castello half an hour ago.'

'What do you mean? You said you hadn't been to the Castello.'

'I could hear you from the beach. You were playing the

piano and then talking to your father.'

He was silent for a moment, and then he said slowly, 'I think you heard a working tape. You see, my father isn't there. He's spending the night with a friend. And I've been out fishing with Adoni.'

'Then why did you attack me?'

'You rushed out onto the path in front of me.'

'Oh, yes. And yet you still held on to me when you knew who I was. Or didn't you want me to see the others?'

'The others?'

'The men who went past when you were holding me.'

'That was Adoni.'

'Well, you needn't worry,' I said. 'I'm not going to tell anyone about you. But I know all about it. I don't care what you do, but I do care about Miranda and her mother, and your father, and Adoni.'

He had listened in silence but now he said very quietly, 'What are you talking about?'

'I suppose poor Yanni didn't do the job last night, so you've been to Albania to do it yourself, haven't you?'

'Where did you get these strange ideas from?'

'Godfrey Manning told me this morning.'

'*What?*' His voice was hard and sharp. I backed away from him, but he quickly took hold of my arm. 'Manning! *He* told you?'

'Let me go, please,' I cried.

He dropped my arm, but said, 'What did Manning tell you?'

'About Yanni? That he was a smuggler, that he probably had a contact, that he hoped the police wouldn't find out because Spiro was in it, too.'

'When did he tell you this?'

'This morning, in the bay, before you came down.'

'Then you weren't up at Manning's house just now?'

'No, of course I wasn't! At this time of night?'

'Of course. I'm sorry. And did Manning tell you that I was Yanni's smuggling contact?'

'No. I decided that myself. I saw Yanni going up to the Castello last night. Anyway, you knew that Yanni was going to go out last night because you weren't surprised when you heard he'd been drowned.'

'You noticed that, did you?'

'Yes, but you were shocked.'

There was a pause, and then he said slowly, 'But you didn't tell the police any of this.' He turned to me. 'My dear, I can't explain, but I must beg you to keep quiet. It's very important. No one must know that I've been out tonight.'

'Don't worry. I won't tell anyone,' I promised. He looked at me. 'Because of Maria and Miranda,' I added quickly, 'and your father.'

There was another short pause. Then he said, 'I'll take you home now. These woods are dark and you were frightened, weren't you?'

'Frightened? No. Of course not.'

'Then why were you running back like that?'

'Because I—' I stopped. The dolphin! I had forgotten the dolphin! 'It was late,' I said. 'I'm all right, really. Good night.'

But he came after me. 'I want to be sure that you get home safely. Anyway, my boat's on your side of the bay. I'd like to move it nearer.'

I was afraid, and he knew it. 'What's the matter?' he

asked. 'Did you meet someone in the bay?'

'No.'

'Then why don't you want me to go down there?'

I said nothing. If I spoke, I would start to cry.

'Look,' he said, 'I have to know. Some day I'll tell you why. Something did happen down there, didn't it?'

'It's the dolphin,' I said weakly.

He stared at me. 'And you still think I want to shoot it? Look, tell me what happened.'

When I had finished explaining, he took hold of my arm again. 'Listen,' he said urgently, 'there's a rope in my boat. I'll go and get it. I'll be quick. Go back to your dolphin and wait for me. Don't worry. We'll save him – but please be very quiet.'

Before I could reply, he had gone.

 8

The rescue

There was no time to think. I obeyed him, and ran back down to the bay. The dolphin wasn't moving, but he was alive and the dark eye watched me. I continued to fetch water to pour over him.

Max Gale came quickly. His little motor-boat slid quietly into the bay, with its engine switched off. He brought the boat in and stepped out, carrying a rope. We tied this round the dolphin and tried to pull him down to the sea. We tried several times – and each time we failed.

'Could we use the boat – tie the rope to it and let the boat

*We tied the rope round the dolphin and tried to pull him
down to the sea.*

pull him out . . . with the engine?' I asked Max desperately.

Max didn't answer immediately and I said, 'It's all right. I understand. You don't want any noise. I'm sorry. I'll stay here all night and keep him wet, and—'

'We'll use the boat,' said Max.

He tied one end of the rope to the boat. The other end was round the dolphin's tail. The engine started with a noise that seemed to fill the night, but the dolphin was not afraid. I stayed with him to make sure he remained the right way up. When he began to slide backwards into the water, I followed him until I was up to my neck in water.

'Oh, Max!' I cried. 'He's so quiet. I think . . . Max, I think he's dead. Oh, Max . . .'

'It's all right, my dear. I'll come. Hold him. We'll float him first.'

'Now!' I called when we reached the deep water, and Max switched off the engine quickly. He came round to me. 'Is he dead?' he asked.

'I don't know, I don't know,' I replied. 'I'll hold him up while you cut the rope.'

'Turn his head towards the sea first,' said Max. He took his knife and bent down to cut the rope. It was difficult and at that moment the dolphin came to life.

'He's all right!' I cried, and suddenly the dolphin pulled out of my arms and swam straight out towards the open sea. Max disappeared under the water and for a moment I thought the dolphin had taken Max with him. For a few seconds the water covered me, too, but when I surfaced again, Max was there by me, holding the cut rope.

I caught his arm. 'Oh, Max, look! There he goes! He's gone! Oh, wasn't it wonderful?'

For the second time that night he took hold of me and silenced me roughly, but this time with his mouth. It was cold, and tasted of salt, and the kiss seemed to last for ever. In the cold water I could feel his body warm against mine.

He let me go, and we stood there, staring at each other.

'Was that my forfeit for the roses?' I managed to whisper.

'Didn't you know how I felt? My father did.' He smiled cheerfully, and moved towards me again.

'Oh, Max,' I cried. 'Not here – in this freezing cold water! It's crazy! Come on out . . . please!'

He laughed, and let me go, but a second later he suddenly took hold of my arm, and I saw a light coming along the path from the Villa Rotha. We had just reached the shore when the light caught us.

'Good heavens! Gale! Lucy! What's happened?' said Godfrey Manning's voice. 'Did you get the diamond, Lucy? Phyl rang me. She was worried. I'd only just got in. What's wrong?'

'Nothing,' said Max, annoyed. He explained about the dolphin.

'You got your boat out at this time of night just to rescue a dolphin?' asked Godfrey. 'But . . . I was sure you went out some time ago.'

'I thought you were out yourself,' replied Max. 'And had only just come in? But, yes, I was out. Adoni went up to the house and I was still in the boat when Miss Waring came.' Then he added, 'We've got to get out of these wet clothes. We'll have to go.'

'Yes,' I said. 'I'll tell you about it when I see you, Godfrey. Thanks for coming down.'

When we were at the foot of the Castello steps, I was going to go past them, but Max put out his hand to stop me.

'You can't go all that way in those wet clothes,' he said. 'Come on up to the house.'

The terrace was empty when we reached the Castello, but one of the long windows was open and Max took me in through this. The room was lit by only one lamp on a low table. Near this Sir Julian was sitting in an armchair. The cat was on his knees. On the table there was a bottle of gin, almost empty, some water and two glasses. Sir Julian was talking to himself – words from *The Tempest*. He was very drunk.

Max stopped just inside the window, and said something quietly. Then I realized that Sir Julian was not alone. Adoni was there.

'Max,' he began, and stopped when he saw me. 'What's happened?' he asked.

'Nothing important,' replied Max. Then he turned to Sir Julian. 'Who's been here, Father?' he said.

'Who's been here?' his father repeated.

'Do you know, Adoni?' Max asked.

'No. I thought the house was empty when I came back. Then I heard voices and found Sir Julian like this, with the tape-recorder on. He did say that his friend, Michael Andriakis, was ill.'

'Someone certainly has been here,' said Max. 'Did he say how he got back from town?' Then he tried again, 'Father, who's been here?'

'I had to ask him to come in,' said Sir Julian. 'He drove me back from town.'

Little by little Max managed to learn from his father that Michael had had a heart attack. There was no telephone in the house, so Sir Julian went for the doctor, and they put

Michael to bed. Then Sir Julian went to fetch Michael's married daughter and her three children, so there was no room for him to stay there. Sir Julian went to the garage to see if someone could drive him home, but just then someone he knew stopped to buy petrol. He offered to drive Sir Julian back. On the way they stopped to buy the gin.

Suddenly Adoni noticed something on the floor and he bent down to pick it up. It was a cigarette end. Adoni showed it to Max and they looked at each other.

'It is, isn't it?' Adoni said.

'Obviously,' replied Max. 'And he let my father get drunk. But he can't have done that deliberately because no one knew about my father's problem, except Michael and us.'

'Perhaps Sir Julian didn't tell him anything,' said Adoni.

'Didn't tell him anything,' repeated Sir Julian happily.

'I'd better get him to bed,' said Max. 'Look after Miss Lucy, will you, Adoni? Show her the bathroom and the spare bedroom. I'm sorry about all this, Lucy.'

I followed Adoni up the wide stairs and we talked about the dolphin. I knew now what Sir Julian's problem was, but my head was full of questions. What were Max and Adoni involved in? They obviously knew who the mysterious visitor was.

I had my bath, put on Sir Julian's dark red silk dressing-gown and went back downstairs. Adoni had promised me a hot drink.

9

Some answers

The door of the music room was open. The lamp was lit, but there was no one there. Just then Max came in. He was wearing clean, dry clothes, and, although he looked tired, he also looked as tough and as purposeful as ever.

'Come on into the kitchen,' he said. 'Adoni and I are having something to eat. And don't worry about your sister. I've rung her to explain. Godfrey Manning had already rung to tell her you'd found her ring, so she's quite happy.'

Max made me sit by the warm fire, and I realized that I was hungry. They gave me hot coffee and a plate of excellent food, cooked by Adoni.

Adoni asked Max if I spoke Greek and, when Max replied that I didn't, Adoni began to talk excitedly in Greek. Then he took three cigarettes from Max, said good night and left the room.

Max and I stayed by the warm fire, and I asked, 'Is your father all right?'

Max looked worried. 'Yes. We've put him to bed, but . . .' He stopped.

'Max,' I said, hesitating, 'I don't think your father told his visitor anything. I think that was why he kept repeating those words from *The Tempest* – to stop him from saying anything else.'

Max smiled at me gratefully. 'Perhaps you're right,' he said. Then he began to talk to me about his father. 'He isn't an alcoholic, you know,' he explained. 'He just drank from time to time to forget. Four years ago my mother and sister were killed in a car accident. My sister was driving and she lived just long enough to know what had happened. Unfortunately, I was in America at the time. I was ill in hospital, and I couldn't get back to be with him and help him through it. It nearly killed him. And that was when he started drinking. It was two months before I got home. He didn't drink all the time – only when everything became too much for him. In the end he had a nervous breakdown. He's better now – or we thought he was. He wants to go back to the theatre, you know, but he won't do it until he's sure that he's all right. And now . . . don't blame him, Lucy.'

'How could I blame him? I love him!'

He smiled. 'Lucy Waring's generous heart. Love given away freely to actors, dolphins . . .' He was suddenly serious. 'Any chance for a musician?'

I was silent, and he looked away, into the fire. 'Sorry. That was rather a sudden question. Forget it.'

But he had asked the question because he wanted the answer. I found my voice again. 'If you'd asked me that three hours ago, I'd have said that I didn't even like you. And now, when . . . when you look at me, my legs go weak. It's never happened to me before . . . and . . . and I'd do anything for you—'

It was an even better kiss this time – the same feeling, but now we were warm and dry.

'And now,' said Max, a little later, 'I'll try to explain to you what this is all about. I'll make it as short as I can. It all starts with Yanni Zoulas—'

'It's true, then? He was a smuggler?'

'Yes. Yanni carried all kinds of things to Albania. He had a contact there, a man called Milo. And there were people over here who gave him things to take – but not me. You know that Albania is a communist country and Russia was ready to help Albania at first. But things didn't go well. There were problems between Albania and Russia, so Albania turned to China for help. Now Albania is closed, except to China, and no one can get in or out.'

'Like Spiro's father?'

'Yes. During the last world war my father and Spiro's father were good friends. My father is the twins' godfather and a godfather is very important here. When Spiro's father disappeared, my father looked after the family. That's why, when Spiro fell off the boat, Maria came to my father. She couldn't believe that Spiro was dead and she wanted my father to find out what had really happened to him, and to bring him back. Obviously, my father couldn't do this himself, so I decided to do it for him. The police knew all about it. They were very helpful and gave me all the information they could. We expected that someone would find Spiro's body in Albania. And then, on Saturday night, when he went on his usual smuggling trip, Yanni had news of Spiro. On Sunday he came to tell us about it.'

I sat up in my chair. 'News of Spiro? Good news?'

'Yes. Spiro is alive. He was found on the beach in Albania by some ordinary people who didn't bother to tell the Albanian police. His leg was broken, but he was alive. Obviously, we had to get him out of the country, and Yanni arranged to get him tonight. He came here to ask me to go with him.'

I stood up. 'You went with Adoni, didn't you? That's what you were doing. You've brought Spiro home?'

Max smiled. 'Yes, we did. He's here now, and he's alive and well.'

'Oh, this is wonderful!' I cried. 'Everyone will be so happy when they know—'

But Max said seriously, 'I'm afraid they mustn't know. When the time comes, we'll say that he was found on an island, but don't you see? Spiro's still in danger. Not from Albania, but from someone here. Don't forget that Yanni is dead.'

I was afraid. 'But we know what happened to Spiro,' I said. 'He fell off Godfrey Manning's boat . . .'

'Lucy,' Max said slowly, 'Godfrey Manning pushed Spiro off the boat, and left him in the sea to drown.'

'Max!' I stared at him. 'I can't believe that. It isn't possible!'

'Spiro has no reason to lie. Remember, I've talked to Spiro, and that's what he says. And Yanni had told us not to tell Godfrey Manning about Spiro.'

'You mean that Godfrey Manning tried to kill Spiro and . . . and that he did kill Yanni? He's a murderer?'

'Well, we're certain about Spiro, but guessing about Yanni. We must talk to Spiro again now. We have to find out why Godfrey Manning was ready to kill two people. And I need your help. I've got to take the boy to Athens tomorrow morning, to the hospital and then to the police. When he's talked to the police, he'll be able to come home. Well, shall we go and see him?'

'Where is he?'

He laughed. 'Below us. He's downstairs in the cellar. Adoni is guarding him.'

10

Spiro

I followed Max down to the cellar. The air was fresh and clean and Max explained that there was a natural cave further along. Suddenly Max stopped, put up his hand to the wall and pulled something. A hole appeared in the wall and Max led me through it. There was a passage which was cut through the rocks. We went down a few more steps. Then, in the light of Max's torch, I saw a face and a gun.

'Adoni? It's Max. I've brought Miss Lucy. Is he all right?'

'He's fine now. He's awake.'

We went into a large cave. Spiro was lying on a very comfortable bed, a warm orange light shone from a lamp, and there was a homely smell of coffee and cigarettes.

Spiro looked surprised when he saw me, but Max said, 'This is Mrs Forli's sister. She's my friend and yours. She's going to help us, and she wants to hear your story.'

Max pulled forward a box so that I could sit down. 'Now,' he said to Spiro, 'if you feel better, try to tell us exactly what happened.'

The boy began to speak slowly. He said that there had been nothing unusual about the trip that night, only that the radio had said that the weather might be bad. He had told Godfrey this, but Godfrey had replied sharply that it would be all right. They had left just before midnight. The night was black, and Godfrey had stayed in the cabin. He had said that he was working on his camera.

'He seemed normal?' Max asked.

Spiro frowned. 'Well, he seemed quiet, and perhaps a bit

sharp with me, but I thought he was still angry with me. Earlier that day I'd gone into the boat-house to service the engine, without asking him first.'

'Go on,' said Max. 'You were out at sea and the night was black . . .'

'I thought we were about half-way across towards Albania,' Spiro continued. 'The weather was getting worse, but Mr Manning didn't want to stop and shelter by the islands. We went on until we were about four kilometres out. He came out of the cabin then, and he sent me in to make some coffee. The camera was there on the table, but the light in the cabin was very bad, and he couldn't have seen well enough to work on the camera. Afterwards, I thought this was strange. It was also strange that we went out to take photographs on such a dark night. And what happened next was even more strange. The engine stopped, but I knew there was nothing wrong with it. I had serviced it myself that morning! But it stopped, and Mr Manning called to me. He was in the back of the boat, and he had hold of the tiller. "I think there's something caught in one of the propellers," he said, and he asked me to look at it. He told me to be careful because the sea was getting rough and the boat was moving about quite a lot. Suddenly the boat swung violently – I thought Mr Manning had turned her across the wind too quickly. But I was holding on to the rail, and I was all right. Then something hit me on the head, from behind. I knew I was going to fall and I put up my arm to save myself. Just then the boat swung round again, and something hit me across the hand. I let go, and fell into the water. When I surfaced, the boat was still quite near. I shouted, not very loudly, but I'm sure he heard me. Then he

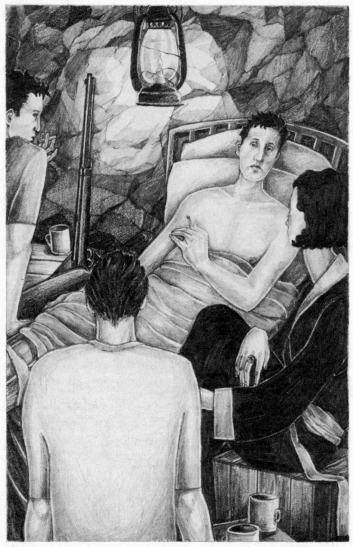

'Go on,' said Max. 'You were out at sea and the
night was black . . .'

shone his torch on me. He saw me! I still didn't know that he'd hit me. I thought it was an accident.'

The injured boy paused, and moved his broken leg in the bed. Then he went on.

'The boat was moving slowly nearer. I called out to Mr Manning, and I began to swim towards him. I saw the starting-handle in his hand, but I thought nothing of it. When I reached the boat, he bent over the side and hit me again. However, because the boat was moving about so much, he only got my arm. He had to hold on to the rail himself, so he couldn't point the torch very well. Then the torch went out and he couldn't see me. At the same time a big wave came, and it carried me away from the boat. This time, of course, I kept quiet. I saw the light go on again, and then the engine started. For a short time he searched for me, but then he turned the boat away and left me there, in the sea.'

There was silence in the cellar. Max's face was cold and hard.

But Spiro had been lucky. He was carried along by the sea to the coast of Albania. There, the sea threw him violently against the rocks, and he broke his leg. Fortunately, an old fisherman found Spiro on the beach, took him home and looked after him.

By the time he had finished his story, Spiro was very tired. Max explained that the next day he would get him to Athens, to hospital. After that they would go and tell the police what had happened. He also promised Spiro that Mr Manning wouldn't know about it.

'The police won't believe me,' Spiro protested.

'But we have to find out why Manning tried to kill you.

Have you any idea why? Do you think it was because you went to service the engine without asking him first?' Max said.

'No.'

'Do you usually ask him first?'

'Of course.'

'But this time you didn't . . . Why did you work on the boat without telling him that morning?' Max wanted to know.

'Mr Manning had asked me if I'd service the engine after breakfast because he was going out in the boat that day. But that morning I went for a swim very early, before breakfast, and I decided to start work then. I knew where he hid the spare key, so I took it and when Mr Manning came down after breakfast I'd nearly finished. I thought he'd be pleased, but he wasn't. He asked me how I got in. I didn't tell him that I knew about the spare key. I just said the door wasn't locked. He'd left his wallet on the boat, and I thought he was angry because he believed I had stolen some of his money. I'm not a thief, and I told him I'd never go to his house again. But then he said he was sorry, and everything was all right again.'

'Did he ask you then to go out with him on the boat that night?' Max said.

'Yes. Earlier he'd said he didn't need me.'

'That was when he decided to kill you, then,' said Max thoughtfully. 'Did you see anything unusual on the boat?' he continued. 'What about the wallet? Were there any papers in it?'

'No, only some foreign money, I think. But I didn't really look.'

'Did Manning leave you alone on the boat after this?' Max asked.

'No,' replied Spiro. 'He asked me to go to the house and help him with some photographs. I worked there all day, and he telephoned my mother and told her that I was going out with him that night.'

'He wanted to be sure that you saw nobody,' Max said. 'All right, Spiro, I'm going to lock you and Adoni in here while I take Miss Lucy home. I'll be back in half an hour. You have the gun, Adoni?'

'Yes,' replied Adoni.

'And this,' added Spiro, and he held up a shining knife.

Adoni followed Max to the door. 'What about Sir Gale?' he asked.

'Oh, he'll sleep now,' said Max. 'And I'll sleep in the kitchen when I come back. Call me if you need me.'

Max and I walked back along the passage. 'Now you understand why Manning mustn't know about Spiro. We've got to find out what he's doing. Yanni suspected that Manning was involved in something and that he wasn't really here just to take photographs and write a book. Perhaps Yanni went to look round the boat-house, and Manning caught him and killed him. He could have put the body in Yanni's boat, taken it out to sea, and left it. Yanni was hit over the head, so it looked like an accident. It was probably also Manning who shot at the dolphin, to keep people away.'

I was shocked and silent. Then I turned to Max. 'What do you want me to do to help?'

'Keep Manning away from Corfu harbour when I bring Spiro back from Athens. I can't fly from the airport on the island. Everybody would know. I'll have to hide Spiro in my car, take the car-ferry across to the mainland, and fly to Athens from there. Tomorrow I'll phone you to tell you what time I'll be back the following day. I'd like to take the ferry that gets back at a quarter past five. Could you have tea with Manning and keep him away from the harbour until after six o'clock?'

'I'll hate it, but I'll do my best,' I said.

11

A difficult afternoon

I slept very late that day. Phyllida woke me when she let the bright sunlight into the room. It was midday.

'It's about time, too,' she said. 'I've brought you some coffee. Oh, yes. Godfrey phoned.'

I sat up quickly, and Phyllida looked surprised. 'What did he want?' I asked.

'He wanted to know if you were safe and had the ring, of course.' Phyllida held up her hand. The diamond ring was back on her finger. 'And what time did you get in? What happened?' she continued.

Quickly I told Phyllida something about the night's events, but not about Spiro, of course, nor about Sir Julian.

Phyllida listened with interest, but then she looked at her watch and cried, 'Good heavens! I'll have to hurry. I'm going into town to have my hair done and to do some shopping. I thought I'd have lunch there, too. Do you want to come with me?'

'When are you leaving?' I asked.

'In about twenty minutes,' she replied.

Just then the phone rang. 'Oh, that'll be Godfrey again. He was going to ask you to have lunch with him, I think. What shall I tell him?'

I said, 'Say I'm in the bathroom and I can't come to the phone, and tell him that I'm going out with you. Ask him to call me tonight.'

'Then you are coming with me?' asked Phyllida.

'No. I'll just rest today, and go to the beach later,' I said.

'OK,' replied my sister, and she went to answer the telephone.

After an early lunch, I told Miranda that I was going down to the bay, and I went to get my swimming things. I wasn't going there, of course, in case Godfrey saw me, but I was hoping to see Adoni in the garden of the Castello to find out if Max and Spiro had got away safely.

But when I came out of my room, Miranda was waiting for me. Adoni had sent a message to say that all was well.

'Did he tell you about the dolphin?' I asked Miranda.

'Yes,' she replied.

'That's all right, then. Thanks, Miranda,' I said, and left the house.

I went towards the woods, and when I got there, I left the path and climbed higher. I sat down in the shade and tried to read my book, but I couldn't. From where I sat I couldn't see the Castello, but I could see the roof of the Villa Rotha. I could also see the Villa Forli in the distance below me. And then I saw what I had expected to see. Godfrey was coming along the path. He didn't go down to the bay, but he stood there looking out towards the sea. He seemed to be looking for someone on the beach or out at sea. He looked towards the Forli house, and, for a moment, I thought he was going to make his way towards it. But he turned and went back along the path.

Soon afterwards I saw his boat slide quietly out of the Castello boat-house where he kept it. Godfrey was at the tiller, and I watched the boat until it disappeared from my view, in the direction of Corfu town.

Max phoned me later. 'Did you get the message from Adoni?' he asked.

'Yes, thank you. He said that all was well. How are you getting on?'

'Well, I'm afraid the police are not very happy about doing anything. They want proof. They don't seem to believe that Manning tried to kill Spiro. They think it was an accident – and Yanni's death, too,' Max explained.

'Well, what about the boy?' I asked. 'Can you bring him home?'

'The hospital says I can, but is it safe? I'm seeing the police again tonight – and there's tomorrow. We can try again then. I hope to be back at a quarter past five.'

'That's all right. Nobody will meet you. I'll make sure of that.'

'Good, but take care of yourself.' His voice was anxious.

'And you,' I replied.

After I put the phone down, I sat there for some time, looking out at the stars in the evening sky. I felt calm and determined. And when the telephone rang again, I didn't even jump. I picked it up.

'Yes? Oh, hello, Godfrey. Yes, it's Lucy . . .'

The next day Godfrey called for me immediately after lunch. He had asked me to have lunch with him, but I knew he only wanted information from me, so I refused. I didn't want to spend too long with him. However, I said that I would love to go for a drive with him in the afternoon. I added that I would like to visit Palaiokastritsa, a famous and beautiful place on the western coast. Godfrey sounded quite happy with this idea.

When we left, we saw Maria outside the villa, and Godfrey waved to her and smiled. She smiled back. Had he really tried to kill her son? I found it difficult to believe now, in the light of day.

It was a very pretty road. I watched the scenery and talked to Godfrey about anything I could think of. But suddenly, I noticed that we had driven past the sign which said 'Palaiokastritsa'. I told Godfrey this, and he replied,

'Oh, yes, I'm sorry. We'll go there one day when I haven't got to be back early.'

'Have you got to be back early?' I enquired.

'Well, yes. I'm afraid I have. I'm going out to dinner with friends tonight,' he said.

'Where are we going, then?' I said.

'To the Achilleion. It's a villa which was built for the Empress of Austria.'

'Oh, that's a wonderful idea!' I replied enthusiastically.

It was a disastrous idea, because, to get there, we had to go through Corfu town – quite close to the harbour – and to come back, we would have to use the same road as Max. I had to make sure that we were not on that road at about half past five. I looked at Godfrey Manning again. He was so calm, and handsome and normal.

Then suddenly he said, 'Now, what happened the night before last at the Castello? Did you see Sir Julian?'

'Well, yes, I did,' I said. 'He was tired,' I added.

'You mean he was drunk,' said Godfrey.

'How do you know that?' I asked.

'Come on, Lucy. They knew I was with him, didn't they? How could I stop him drinking if he wanted to?' He gave a little smile, but there was something about his mouth that was both cruel and frightening.

Suddenly I knew. Of course he was a murderer. I no longer had any doubts.

'Well, Mr Gale isn't very pleased with you,' I said.

'I suppose not,' Godfrey Manning replied. 'Where is he today?'

'Oh, Athens, I think. But tell me what happened with you and Sir Julian,' I continued quickly.

'Nothing, really. The old man needed someone to take him home, and I wanted to talk to him. I wanted to find out what I could about Spiro. Everybody on this island tells the Gales everything – but Spiro's death involves me, too,' he said.

'And did Sir Julian have any news?' I asked.

'No. Did the Gales say anything to you when you were at the Castello?'

'Nothing.'

'Did they say anything about Yanni Zoulas?'

'Yanni? . . . Oh, the fisherman who was drowned . . . No, why?'

'Oh, I was just curious.'

'Well, if there is any news about Spiro, Maria will tell my sister, and we'll tell you,' I said.

We drove on for a time in silence. It was obvious that Godfrey wanted to know if anyone suspected that the two deaths were not accidents. Perhaps he still had some 'business' to finish. Well, he'd learn nothing from me.

Soon we arrived at the Achilleion. 'Well, here we are,' said Godfrey, and we stopped outside the palace. I made him look at everything, inside and in the gardens, and from time to time I studied the little guide book I had brought with me. I had to keep him there as long as I could. But at half past four we had seen everything, and Godfrey asked me if I would like to go to Corfu town, where we could get a cup of tea.

'Oh, no,' I said quickly. 'Isn't there anywhere to have tea in the other direction? The coast that way looks so beautiful.'

We had tea in a little hotel on the beach, and I pretended to be very interested in everything around me. I told him how much I enjoyed watching the boats on the sea, and we stayed there quite a long time. Suddenly Godfrey said, 'Oh, look! There's the ferry.'

'Ferry?' I replied. 'What ferry?' With some difficulty, I managed to keep my voice calm and unworried.

'The boat that goes between Corfu and the mainland,' he answered. 'It'll be in Corfu in about twenty minutes. Well, shall we go?'

'I'd like to go upstairs first, please,' I said.

The owner of the hotel led me to a bathroom, where I feverishly studied my guide book. Ah, yes – the place where Menecrates was buried. I would ask Godfrey to take me there. It was on the way back.

He did take me there, and it was a wonderful idea because

*We asked everybody we met where Menecrates was buried,
but nobody knew.*

nobody knew where it was. We asked everybody we met, and they all sent us to the wrong place. Godfrey thought I just didn't want to leave him! When we finally found it, it was after six o'clock.

'Would you like to come and have a drink with me before I take you home?' Godfrey asked.

'That would be lovely,' I said.

12

A discovery

It was quite dark when Godfrey drove me back to the Villa Forli. Phyl was out, but she had left me a note. She said that Leo was coming to Corfu with the children for two weeks, so she had gone to Corfu town to do some shopping. I read the note, and just then Miranda came in and said that Phyllida had phoned. She had met some friends in town and she was having dinner with them at the Corfu Palace Hotel. Miranda had also heard from Adoni that Max would be late and would not be on the ferry which arrived at a quarter past five.

Miranda was different – excited and happier. She seemed to want to tell me something. Finally I said, 'Miranda, what is it? Something's happened. Can you tell me about it?' I hoped desperately that Adoni had kept his promise not to tell her about Spiro.

She was silent for a moment and then she said, 'Adoni and I – we found it together this afternoon. I had some free time, so I went to find Adoni. They said he was swimming in the

bay, and I went down to look for him. I saw him coming out
of a cave, in the cliff under Mr Manning's villa. At first he
wasn't very pleased to see me, but then he took me into the
cave and showed me what he'd found. In the water at the
bottom of the cave there were some books. They were in
foreign writing and there were pictures. They were covered
with little stones, but you could see under the stones. Adoni
said they were proof.' Miranda's eyes were wide with
wonder.

'Proof of what?' I stared at her, my heart beating fast.

'That all the stories about Saint Spiridion and his magic
books are true! Adoni didn't explain, and he said it must be
a secret until he has talked to Mr Max.'

Clearly, Adoni had invented some 'magic' explanation for
Miranda, but the word 'proof' to me meant only one thing.
Adoni must have found something to connect Godfrey
Manning with the murders.

'Well, Miranda,' I said, 'that's very exciting news. I think
I'll telephone the Castello now and ask Adoni about it.'

'But there's no one there,' she said. 'Sir Julian has gone
out to have dinner with a friend, and Adoni has gone to the
harbour to meet Mr Max from the ferry at eleven o'clock.'

Of course, Adoni would tell Max. But then I remembered
that Godfrey Manning was also going out tonight. Perhaps
when Max and Adoni came back with the police, this
'proof' that Adoni had found would no longer be there.
There was only one thing to do. I stood up.

'Will you show me this cave and these books, now,
Miranda?' I asked. My voice was urgent.

'Now?' she repeated, surprised. 'But it's so dark!'

'Please, Miranda,' I begged. 'Don't ask me to explain, but

I must go now. It's very important. Just show me the cave.'

'Well, of course, Miss Lucy,' Miranda replied. 'But what would happen if Mr Manning came down? Adoni seemed worried about Mr Manning.'

'He won't. He's out. He told me so. But we'll phone his house to make sure.'

I called the Villa Rotha, but there was no reply.

'Shall I get the torch, Miss Lucy?' Miranda asked.

'Yes, please. I'll get my coat and change my shoes, and you put a coat on, too.'

Three minutes later I was ready and I had taken Leo's gun from his room.

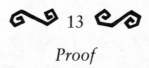

13

Proof

The bay was dark and silent. We crossed the beach and made our way towards the path which led up to the Villa Rotha. Miranda went first, and suddenly she stopped in front of some bushes which grew against the cliff. She pulled them to one side, and I saw a small opening and a passage which led down. Miranda went in first because she knew the way, and I followed her. The passage turned left and right, and at the end of it we came to some natural steps in the rock. They went down to a kind of shelf, which ran round a long cave with a pool of black water at the bottom of it.

'Down there!' said Miranda urgently. 'Shine the torch down there,' she repeated, pointing to the water.

It was there! And there were stones on top of it to hide it. But to me it looked more like a box than books. Just then I heard a noise. I switched off the torch quickly. 'Keep very still,' I whispered to Miranda. 'Listen!'

The sound came again – a careful footstep somewhere in the passage above. He was coming!

'Quick!' I whispered. 'We must hide.'

Slowly, carefully, almost without a sound, we moved back behind the rocks.

And then the cave was filled with light. We heard a man's breathing, and the sound of something going into the water. More noises. Things were being pulled from the pool. At last the light moved away and we were left in blackness.

'Wait,' I whispered to Miranda. I went back to the pool and looked down into the water. There was nothing there. The 'proof' had gone! I had to follow him! I went back to Miranda.

'It's all right,' I said. 'You can come out now.'

'What was it?' she asked, and now she was afraid.

'The books have gone, and it was Mr Manning who took them. I have to see where he puts them, but he mustn't see us. I'll explain later. Do you understand, Miranda? He mustn't see us. Come on!'

We made our way slowly back up the steps and along the passage. We kept stopping to listen, in case Manning was still there. But soon we reached the entrance to the cave. We didn't dare to follow the path because we didn't want Manning to see us, so we moved carefully through the bushes. There was no moon, but the sky was full of stars.

We stopped just above the boat-house. I thought that the door was open, but I couldn't quite see. But then I heard the sound of a door closing. A dark shadow moved silently across the boat-house wall and then he came quietly up the path. We lay very still, and I saw him quite clearly.

'You saw who it was, Miranda?' I whispered.

'Of course,' she replied. 'It was Mr Manning. But, Miss Lucy, what is happening?'

I started to explain to her. 'Look, Miranda, Mr Max and I think . . . things have been happening . . . we think that they are connected with Spiro's accident. Adoni thinks so, too. It's serious, and it might be dangerous. Will you help me?'

'Yes . . . Look! Up there!' Miranda was pointing to the top of the cliff. A light had gone on in the Villa Rotha.

'I wish I could get into that boat-house,' I said. 'I think Mr Manning's put the things from the cave in there. He said he was going out, but perhaps that wasn't true . . . Perhaps he's going out with the boat later. And then it'll be too late. Anyway, the boat-house is locked.'

'I know where the spare key is,' said Miranda. 'Spiro showed me.'

Just then the lights in the villa went out, and I heard the sound of Godfrey's car. Then I saw its lights disappear into the distance, and it was dark again.

I pushed my hand down into the pocket of my coat and felt the hardness of Leo's gun. I didn't want to go near Godfrey Manning's boat-house – but I had to.

'Come on,' I said to Miranda, and we ran down the path. 'When we've got the key,' I said, 'you must go straight back to the Castello. Then you'll see them as soon as they get home. But try to telephone Adoni first . . . Do you know where he could be?'

'Yes. There are two bars where he sometimes eats.'

We had reached the boat-house and Miranda ran to find the spare key. She pushed it into my hand. 'What shall I tell Adoni?' she asked.

'Just say he must come straight back here. Miss Lucy says it's urgent. Then wait for him. Lock the door and don't let anyone else in, except Max or the police. If I'm not back when Adoni comes, tell him everything and say that I'm down here. All right?'

'Yes,' Miranda answered immediately. She turned and ran quickly up the path.

I looked up at the dark Villa Rotha and then, with a trembling hand, I put the key in the lock. The door opened and I went inside.

All round the boat-house there was a kind of narrow wooden platform. There was nowhere to hide except on the boat itself. At the back of the boat-house there was a window, and from this I could just see part of the Villa Rotha. If Godfrey did come back, I would see the lights and know that he was there. I stepped onto the boat and tried the cabin door. It wasn't locked. I looked through the window to make sure that I was still safe, and then I went into the cabin. I shone my torch round it and then I began my search. I looked everywhere – in every cupboard, corner, and container; under the beds, in the little kitchen. I found nothing. There were two doors in the floor, one under the table and one at the front of the boat. I pulled them both open and looked below – but there was nothing.

Quickly I ran back to look through the boat-house window at the Villa Rotha again. It was still in darkness. I could search for a little longer.

I started on the deck, and I searched every possible hiding-place – and still I found nothing. I had looked everywhere that I could think of and I stood on the deck, wondering where to look next. Suddenly I saw the answer – a trail of wet drops across the deck, drops of water from a wet packet. Of course! I followed them back into the cabin and over to the table. On the table there was still a wet square where he had put the packet down. There were no more drops of water, because Godfrey must have opened the door under the table. But I had looked there already, and found nothing.

Once again I pulled open the door and looked down into the square hole. I knelt down, switched on the torch and stared down into the water lying in the bottom of the boat. Nothing. I lay down and put my head through the hole – and they were there! They were on a special shelf under the floorboards and just above the water. They were some way back from the opening and you had to lie down to see them.

I ran back to the window. The Villa Rotha was still in darkness.

In two minutes I had one of the packets in my hand. It was wrapped in plastic and it was difficult to see what was inside – a picture, some words.

Somewhere something banged. I jumped in terror and dropped the torch. I picked it up quickly and swung round to look. There was nothing – only darkness.

'It must have been the wind,' I thought. The door banged again. I'd had enough. Holding the packet carefully, I climbed out of the boat.

At that moment I saw a movement on the path outside the window. It was only a shadow – but it was him, and he was coming towards the boat-house fast.

At that moment I saw a movement on the path outside the window.

I had to hide the packet! He'd already murdered one person and tried to kill another because of it. There was only one place – down the side of the boat. Wildly, I tried to push it down into the water, but the boat was too close to the platform and the packet wouldn't go down. I tried again, and this time I heard the packet fall into the water. At the same time Leo's gun slid from the pocket of my coat, and followed the packet into the water.

I heard Godfrey's key in the door. I had to hide. But where? The only place was in the cabin. Quickly and silently, I slipped back into the cabin and ran over to the bed. I lay down and pulled up all the blankets over me. I lay still – and hoped that he wouldn't come into the cabin.

I could feel him moving about the boat. The wind was stronger now and the boat was rocking more. I heard the sound of metal and I could smell the sea air – and suddenly I realized what he'd done. He had taken the boat out of the boat-house and we were out at sea.

I couldn't move. I tried to think. Max and Adoni would come home, they would find that the boat had gone, and they would guess that I was on it. I hoped that Godfrey wouldn't discover the packet had gone, because then he would search the boat and he would find me. I must stay where I was. Perhaps the wind would keep Godfrey on deck. Perhaps he wouldn't come down to the cabin at all.

Just three minutes later, he opened the cabin door.

14

The moment of truth

I heard the door close again. Then I heard the sound of a match and I smelt the smoke of a cigarette which had just been lit. This must be why he had come in. Now he would go away again.

But he didn't. I could feel that he was standing very near me. He stayed there for a few seconds, but to me it seemed to be much longer. Then he left.

It was very hot under the blankets, but I waited for a few moments until I was sure he had gone, and then very slowly and carefully, I began to push back the blankets. I had to find a weapon. I moved the blankets again – and then I froze with horror. My foot, in its bright yellow shoe, was not hidden. Godfrey Manning must have seen it, and now he would do – what?

I soon had my answer because I heard him switch on the engine and the boat stopped rocking. He had turned the boat into the wind and had not taken in the sail. He wouldn't need to stay on deck to look after the boat now. He was already coming towards the cabin door.

I jumped off the bed, dropped my wet coat and put my dress straight. When Godfrey Manning entered the cabin, I was looking for the matches to light the lamp.

I called to him cheerfully over my shoulder. 'Hello. I hope you don't mind a stowaway?'

I lit the lamp, and Manning said, 'I'm delighted, of course. How did you know I'd decided to come out in the boat?'

'Oh, I didn't. I just hoped that you would.'

His voice and manner were as pleasant as usual. I noticed that there was a mirror on a cupboard door, and I pretended to tidy my hair.

'What made you come down to the boat-house?' he asked.

'Well, I wanted a walk after supper, and – have you got a comb, Godfrey? My hair looks awful.'

He said nothing, but he took a comb from his pocket and gave it to me. His eyes were as hard as stones.

'Well, I went down to the beach,' I continued. 'I was looking for the dolphin. Anyway, I went to look, but it wasn't there. I walked along the path a bit, and then I heard you over at the boat-house, so I hurried. I hoped you were going out.'

'You heard me at the boat-house?'

'Yes. I heard the door.'

'When was this?'

'Oh, I'm not sure. About half an hour ago, I think. I was going to call to you, but you were hurrying, so—'

'You saw me?'

He was right behind me now, so I turned quickly, gave him back his comb, and sat down.

'Yes, I did,' I replied. 'You were coming out of the boat-house and then you rushed up the path to the house.'

He realized that I hadn't seen him coming from the cave with the packets, and his small frown disappeared. 'And then?' he said.

I smiled at him brightly. 'I was going to call you then, but I knew from the clothes you were wearing that you must be going out in the boat. I decided to wait until you came back and ask you then.'

'Why didn't you?'

I looked ashamed. 'Well, I'm sorry . . . It was just that you were a long time . . . and I was bored. I tried the boat-house door and it was open, so—'

'The door was open?' His face was still hard and watchful.

'Yes. I think the lock isn't very good. I heard you lock it, so I was quite surprised when it opened. I'm sorry,' I said again, 'but I was sure you wouldn't mind—'

'Then why did you hide?'

'Well, it was awful, really.' I was using every bit of my acting experience now. 'I was looking round – a boat is interesting, different from a house, and when I heard you coming, well, I was ashamed. I'm really sorry. Please don't be angry with me,' I begged. I wondered if I should try a few tears, but decided on an anxious smile instead.

'I'm not angry,' replied Godfrey, and he smiled. Then he turned me round and kissed me.

I tried to pretend that it was Max, but it was no good. I watched the lamp swinging just behind Godfrey's head. If I could make Godfrey move nearer to it . . . But just then the boat rocked violently and Godfrey rushed out of the cabin. In a few moments he was back, and he held out his hand to me. 'Come out and see the stars,' he said. 'Here, take my coat. It's warmer than yours.'

Quickly, I took the torch out of my own coat pocket and put it into the pocket of the coat he gave me.

Outside it was windy, but the stars still shone in the night sky. In the distance I could see a few lights along the dark coast. 'Come on over here and sit next to me,' said Godfrey. And he pulled me down beside him at the back of the boat. I thought that he probably had a gun, so when he kissed me again, I tried to feel for it. It wasn't in his left pocket certainly. I looked desperately over his shoulder. I must find something to hit him with. And then I saw my weapon. The boat's flare, which was made of metal. It was hanging on the side of the boat, but I couldn't reach it.

'Poor Lucy,' said Godfrey, still holding me tightly, 'I'm sorry I was so awful to you.' And then he added carelessly, 'Where's Phyl tonight? Does she know you're out?'

'She's out with friends at the Corfu Palace,' I said, 'but Miranda was in the house. I told her I was coming out.'

'To the boat-house?'

'Well, no. I didn't know that myself, did I?'

I had no way of knowing if Godfrey believed my story or not. If he didn't, he would probably kill me. Perhaps I could get him to stop watching me for a moment. Then I could get the flare.

'Listen!' I said suddenly. 'What's the matter with the engine?'

He turned his head. 'It sounds all right to me. It must be that other boat over there. The wind's carrying the sound this way.'

I stared out over the black water. There was a light in the distance, but no one would hear me if I called.

'Oh! Look at that, Godfrey!' There was a bright green light and a huge fish moved through the water. 'Oh, please, Godfrey, let's take a photograph—'

'No. Stay here.' His arm was like iron. 'I want to ask you something.'

'What?' I said.

'Why did you come tonight?'

'But I told you—'

'Do you expect me to believe you? I've kissed women before, and I know you didn't come because you wanted to be with me.'

'Well,' I laughed uncomfortably. 'I didn't expect you to go to work on me so fast. I'm sorry. Now I feel stupid. It's my fault. Perhaps you'd better take me home.'

'No, my dear.' His voice was different now. 'You're here now, and you're going to stay. You're going all the way.'

'But, you can't want me—' I began.

'I don't,' he replied. 'You came because you wanted to, and now you're staying because I say you have to. Anyway, I haven't got time to take you back. I'm on an urgent trip tonight—'

'Godfrey—'

'I'm taking a lot of forged money to Albania. It's under the cabin floor. If they catch me, they'll shoot me. Do you understand?'

'But why would you do that?' I gasped.

'If you flood a country with forged money, the value of its own money falls, and then the government falls, too. Trouble like that gives a stronger country the chance to move in. Now do you understand?'

I did. Everything was now horribly clear. 'How long have you been doing this?' I asked.

'Oh, for some time. This is the last trip. Then G. Manning will disappear.' He added, 'It's a pity I can't use those photographs of Spiro, though. We'll soon reach the place where I threw him over the side.'

There was no change in his voice, and he still held me

tightly with one arm. The sails banged in the wind and I jumped. Godfrey laughed.

'Who's paying you?' I asked.

'Well, it isn't Greece,' he answered. 'What would you say if I told you that I was being paid twice?'

'I'd say it was pity that you couldn't be shot twice,' I replied. 'Anyway, who makes the forged money?' I added.

'Oh, someone who used to work for Leo.'

'Leo?' I was shocked. 'I can't believe—'

'Oh, Leo isn't involved in this. He knows nothing about it – but if anything had gone wrong, and they knew the money came from here, Leo would have been the suspect – not me. Clever, eh?'

'And Spiro found out?'

'I don't think so, but there was a chance he'd seen a sample in my wallet.'

'And you killed him – just on a chance!' I said fiercely. 'How do people get to be like you? You're a traitor and a murderer. You don't care how many people you destroy. Why do you do it? You don't need the money. It isn't for political reasons. Is it because cheap little criminals like you can't get excitement any other way?'

'Exactly that,' he replied, but I felt a movement of anger through his body.

'And now what are you going to do?' I asked. 'Throw me into the sea?'

'When I do,' he said, 'you'll be glad to go.'

And then he stood up. He swung round towards me and his hands reached for my throat. Wildly I felt for the torch, and found it. The boat gave a violent movement, his foot slipped and his hands missed. I was up against the side of the boat and this time his hands caught my throat. His fingers held it tightly. I pulled my left hand free and hit him in the face with the torch. I didn't hit him very hard, and he still had his hands round my throat, but he had to step back. I kicked the tiller hard with my left foot and the boat turned round with the speed of a bullet. The boom swung towards his head with great force. But he saw it coming. He bent down and caught it on his arm, and the violent movement of the boat threw his body against mine. The boat swung again, and together we slid across the deck. At first I thought that Manning was dead, but then his head moved, and I saw his face, half-covered with blood. He was trying to get his gun. I managed to pull down the metal flare and I began to move towards him. I raised the flare.

It was too late. The gun was in his hand. He lifted it and fired. I bent down and jumped over the side of the boat into the sea.

I was coughing, swallowing salt water and gasping, but I fought the cold, black sea, and finally I surfaced. Everything around me was black, and I went down again. The cold water closed over me, and this brought me back to consciousness. Godfrey Manning had missed me when he fired, but I realized that he would search for me to make sure that I was dead.

Just then a wave caught me and lifted me. I saw Manning's boat. It was going round in circles, searching for me. I knew that Manning would continue to look until he found me.

Then, not far away, I saw the light of another boat – the boat we had seen earlier. It was coming nearer to see what the strange light was in its fishing waters.

I kicked the tiller hard with my left foot.

Manning turned his boat away and the sound of its engine was soon lost in the distance.

Then I shouted.

My cry for help was too weak. There was no reply.

Suddenly I realized that I was being carried towards the shores of Corfu. When I jumped from the boat, we were not as near to Albania as when Manning threw Spiro over the side. I remembered that Yanni's body had been carried back to the Villa Rotha. Saint Spiridion was taking care of me.

But twenty minutes later I knew that I couldn't do it. The sea was pulling me down, the waves were driving into my eyes, my mouth. I couldn't breathe, or see . . . I was drowning . . .

Suddenly, someone very strong seemed to lift me, and half throw me through the waters. Gasping and coughing, I came up out of the blackness, and was thrown forward again. Then a huge wave took me forwards, and rolled me up the beach.

I dug my fingers into the sand to stop the sea pulling me back, and looked round to see who my rescuer was. I saw his shining black body rise from the waves and then he turned on his tail and was gone.

I fell unconscious on the sand, just above the edge of the sea.

15

Back from the dead

When I opened my eyes, I saw a light shining above me. It was a lamp in the window of a little house near the top of the cliffs. I was lucky because there was a path going up towards it. Somehow I managed to reach the path and I started to pull myself up it, in the direction of the light.

I found myself in a narrow valley with the lights of the little houses shining through the trees. I stopped for a moment to rest, and then I moved forwards again. A moment later I tripped and fell. I cried out and immediately a dog began to bark. The door of one of the little houses opened and a stream of light fell across the grass. A man stood at the door and stared out into the darkness.

'Please,' I gasped in English, 'please – help me.' I went forward with my arms stretched out in front of me, and fell, unconscious, at the feet of the man who had opened the door.

He called his wife and I was lifted and carried into the house. Then the old man left the room and his wife took off my clothes and put them to dry by the fire. Gently, she wrapped me in a blanket, made me sit by the fire and gave me a bowl of hot soup. When the man came back, they tried to ask me questions, but I couldn't understand their language. 'English,' I said. 'I'm English.' Two more men came into the room, their sons, and one of them spoke German. My German was very bad, but I managed to tell them I was from the Castello dei Fiori and that I wanted to get back there.

No one in the little village had a car, of course.

'Telephone?' I asked.

There was a telephone in the village, and the men went out again while I got dressed. The old lady would not let me put on my own wet clothes, but proudly brought out the beautiful national dress of Corfu, which she made me put on.

There were now sixteen men waiting outside to help me. They took me up to the village shop where the telephone was. They woke up the shopkeeper, who was delighted to help.

However, when I rang the Castello there was no reply. I hesitated, and then decided to try the Villa Forli.

Phyllida answered immediately. 'Lucy! Where are you?'

'I'm all right, Phyl. Don't worry. But please do as I ask. It's very important. Ring Godfrey. If he answers, tell him I'm not home yet, and ask if I'm with him. Say that you're worried. Please, Phyllida. Do it. Don't ask any questions. I must know if he's home. When you've done it, ring me back here.' I gave her the number.

'However did you get there?' she asked. 'Did Godfrey—'

'I'll explain when I get back, but he did leave me to get home alone. I don't like him, Phyl.'

'Do you want me to come for you?' she asked.

'Perhaps,' I said. 'But call me back when you've phoned Godfrey.'

'All right,' she said. 'I'll call you again in a minute.'

By now there were twenty-three men in the village shop – and they were all smiling. One of them spoke to me in German again. 'Come,' he said.

Outside, in front of the shop, there was a motor-cycle.

A young man was sitting on it proudly.

'He comes from the next village,' said the man who spoke German. 'He's been to visit his uncle. He'll take you home.'

I felt tears in my eyes.' You're all so kind,' I managed to say. 'Thank you.'

It was all I could say in their language, but it seemed to be enough. The air was filled with the warmth of their kindness.

Just then the telephone rang, and I ran back to answer it.

'Lucy? He isn't there. Do you want me to come for you?' Phyllida asked.

'No, thanks, Phyl. I have a friend who's going to bring me home. But don't say anything to anyone.'

When we reached the Castello, I tried to thank the young man. He replied with a few words which clearly meant that it was a pleasure to help me.

Just before he left, I put out my hand and touched his. 'Your name?' I said in Greek.

'Spiridion,' he answered. And the next second he had gone.

There was no light in the Castello, and the house looked huge in the darkness. But I could see a light coming from the Villa Rotha. I moved quietly through the woods, towards the light, and I almost fell over Godfrey's car. It was hidden under the trees. Manning had put the car there so that people would think he had gone out in it. In front of the villa there were two more cars – Max's car and one I didn't recognize. 'Perhaps it's the police,' I thought.

I made my way onto the terrace and moved slowly towards the french windows.

'I have a friend who's going to bring me home.'

The curtains were not properly closed, so, from where I was standing, I could see into the room. There was a hole in the glass where someone had broken into the house, so I could hear what the people in the room were saying.

The first person I saw was Godfrey. He was sitting by the window, near a big wooden desk. He looked very calm, and he had a glass of whisky in his hand. I was delighted to see that there was a very bad bruise on one side of his face. It was covered with dried blood and his mouth seemed to hurt when he drank.

At first the room seemed to be full of people. Not far from Godfrey, in the middle of the floor, Max was standing. He was half turned away from me, and I couldn't see his face. Adoni was over by the door. He was facing the windows, but he was looking at Godfrey. Near me, on one side of my window, was Spiro. He was sitting on the edge of a low chair with his broken leg, in plaster, stretched out in front of him. Miranda was sitting on the floor next to him. Also on the floor, by the boy's chair, there was a gun, and his hand was hanging near it. The police must have told him to put it down.

Over by the door, on the other side of the room from Godfrey, there was a policeman sitting on a chair. I recognized him because he was the Inspector from Corfu town who had enquired into Yanni's death. He looked uncertain, and Godfrey was speaking to him in a light, untroubled voice.

'You see, Mr Papadopoulos, I'm not happy about what happened in my boat-house, and these two men broke into my house. I'm not ready to forget this. If they hadn't phoned for the police, I would have done so. And I know nothing about the girl. I've told you everything we did this afternoon and there are many people who saw us.'

'It's tonight we're interested in.' Max's voice was rough and angry. 'What happened to your face?'

'An accident,' replied Godfrey coldly.

'Please, Max,' said the Inspector. 'Now, Mr Manning, when did you last see Miss Lucy Waring?'

'I took her home at seven o'clock, before dinner, and I haven't seen her since then. I had to go out again this evening, you see.'

'And when you went down to the boat-house, it was locked, and there was nobody there?'

'That's right.'

'What about what this girl said?'

'Miranda? She'd say anything. Her brother seems to have some strange ideas about me.'

Max was about to say something, but the Inspector stopped him. 'We'll come back to that later,' he said, 'when Petros comes back from his search of the boat-house.'

The Inspector turned to Godfrey, 'When Mr Gale met you on your return, you told him that it had been a "normal" trip. What exactly did you mean? Were you out taking photographs?'

'If I say that I was taking photographs, you'll look at my cameras, and you'll know that it isn't true. I went over to the other side.' Godfrey was very calm.

Everybody waited for him to continue. 'He's going to tell them!' I thought. 'But why?'

And then I saw what he was doing. He wanted to give the police some fairly innocent explanation to stop them from finding out the truth.

'Where on the other side?' asked the Inspector.

'Albania.'

'And what were you doing there?'

'Smuggling.'

'You admit this?'

'Of course. You know it goes on all the time – Yanni Zoulas, for example.'

'You know something about his death?'

'No.' Clearly Godfrey had wanted to bring in Yanni's name before someone else did.

'What was Zoulas's connection with you?'

'With me? None.'

'You didn't kill him because he found out something about you—'

I didn't hear what came after this, because just then I saw the policeman coming up from the boat-house.

'Should I tell him about the packet?' I wondered, but then I decided that he probably didn't understand English.

I turned back to the window. Godfrey was pretending to be angry now. 'Perhaps you could tell me why I should possibly want to murder somebody?' he said to Papadopoulos.

'Look,' Max said, 'at the moment it's the girl who's important—'

'Just a minute,' said Papadopoulos. He pulled open the door and the policeman came into the room.

But he had obviously not found the packet. I moved nearer to the window and Adoni saw me. His eyes met mine across the room. Everybody else was looking at the policeman, except Spiro, whose eyes never left Godfrey. Adoni left the room quietly and nobody noticed. I moved back from the window and went round the corner of the house.

A voice whispered in the darkness, 'Miss Lucy! Miss Lucy! I thought . . . I couldn't believe . . . these clothes. But it is you! We thought you were dead!' Somehow I was in his arms and he was holding me. 'We thought you'd gone with that murderer in his boat and that he'd killed you!'

'I did go with him, and he did try to kill me, but I got away,' I managed to reply.

'We've got to get him now,' Adoni said fiercely.

'We will,' I promised. 'I know everything now, and he's not only a murderer. He's a traitor and a paid spy, and I can prove it.'

'Come in now, Miss Lucy, and tell the Inspector,' said Adoni. 'There's no need to be afraid of Manning. I thought Max was going to kill him. He's been so worried about you.'

'Wait a minute, Adoni. What's happened? These are the Corfu police, aren't they? Didn't anyone come from Athens?' I asked.

'No,' replied Adoni. 'They said we must bring Spiro home, and then see the Corfu police tomorrow morning. They didn't seem to be very interested. So Max and Spiro came back alone, and I met the ferry. I told Max about the cave and the packet and he decided to drive home quickly and go to the cave himself.'

'Then you didn't get my message from Miranda?'

'No. She telephoned the Corfu Bar, but I hadn't been in there. They sent a boy to look for me, but he couldn't find me. I had supper with a friend at his house, and then I went to wait for the ferry. When we got to the Castello, Miranda was waiting for us. After a time she remembered, and told us about you.'

'After a time?'

'Well, there was Spiro, you see.' Adoni smiled.

'Of course,' I said. 'That would make her forget everything else.'

'When she told us, Max and I ran down to the boat-house. I've never seen him like that before! We searched everywhere for you, and then we went up to the Villa Rotha. It was locked, so Max broke the window. When we couldn't find you, Max phoned Mr Papadopoulos at his home. He asked him to bring Miranda and Spiro from the Castello, too. Then Max and I went back to the boat-house to wait for Mr Manning.'

'Yes?' I said.

'Well, after some time he came and Max attacked him. "Where's my girl?" he cried. I think Max wanted to kill him. But the police came then. Miss Lucy, you said we could get Mr Manning. Is it true?'

Quickly I told Adoni my story and what I knew about Godfrey. 'The Athens police will have to do something about the forged money, of course,' I added. 'But we must get the police to stop Manning from leaving.'

'What about the proof?' asked Adoni. 'You said you had proof.'

'I've got a packet of the money,' I said. 'I hid it in the water in the boat-house. Godfrey Manning must know now that I took it and he's probably guessed that I hid it there. I'll go inside now, but you go and get the proof. It's about half-way along on the left-hand side. Manning's a dangerous man. He'll probably try to kill me if he thinks I'm the only person who knows where the money is. Go now, Adoni.'

'All right,' he said, 'but be careful.'

'Did you take Manning's gun from him?' I asked.

'Yes, but the police took it from us.'

'Right,' I said. 'Let's go.'

The only difference in the room was that the policeman had taken Adoni's place by the door. By now Godfrey had told the police that he had been smuggling radios.

'But can't all this wait until the morning?' Godfrey asked the Inspector. 'If the girl really is missing, you should be looking for her. That's more important.'

The Inspector and Max began to speak together, but suddenly Miranda cried out, 'He knows where she is! He's killed her! He tried to kill my brother.'

Godfrey banged his hand down on the desk. 'For the last time, I tell you, I don't know where she is! I haven't seen her since I took her home at seven o'clock.'

No actress ever had a better entrance line. I pulled the window open, and went into the room.

 16

The last act

For a moment no one moved. I was watching Godfrey. Max was about to rush forward, but Papadopoulos stopped him.

I said, 'I don't suppose you were expecting me, Godfrey.'

He didn't speak, and there was no colour in his face. He stepped backwards, with his hand stretched out towards the desk.

'Oh, Lucy, my dear,' said Max.

The Inspector spoke. 'It is Miss Waring, isn't it? I didn't know you for a moment, in those clothes. We have been wondering where you were.'

I noticed that Petros, the policeman, had a gun. I replied, 'Yes. I've been listening. I wanted to hear what Mr Manning would say, and I wanted to find out what had been happening since I left him an hour or so ago.'

'We were right!' said Max.

'An hour ago?' repeated the Inspector. 'You were with Mr Manning in his boat an hour ago?'

Petros had moved forward from the door, with his gun in his hand. Godfrey was supporting himself on the desk, and his face was still white.

Max said, 'Look at his face! He tried to kill you?'

'Yes,' I said.

'Max, please!' Papadopoulos warned. 'Now then, Miss Waring, tell us your story, please.'

'Yes, of course. But first there's something urgent I must tell you—'

Suddenly the telephone rang, and the policeman with the gun made an automatic movement towards it.

Godfrey moved like lightning. The hand which was supporting him on the desk moved lower, opened a drawer, raised a gun, and fired – all in a tenth of a second.

Petros's gun answered, but it was too late. Manning's bullet hit Petros in the arm and knocked the gun from his hand. Petros's bullet went into the wall behind the desk, and Petros fell back against Max as Max rushed forward.

In the same second Godfrey jumped towards the open window. I felt my arm caught in an iron hand, and Godfrey pulled my body back against him. I could feel his gun in my side.

'*Keep back*!' he shouted.

Max was half-way across the room, but he stopped immediately. Papadopoulos, who was rising from his chair, stayed where he was. Petros was by the wall, blood flowing through the fingers which held his wounded arm.

'I'm leaving now,' said Manning, 'and the girl is going with me. If you try to follow me, I'll kill her. Oh, no. I'm not taking her with me all the way. She's caused me enough trouble already! You can come down for her when you hear the boat leave – not before. Do you understand?'

He pulled me backwards towards the window.

Max said desperately, 'He won't leave her, Papadopoulos. He'll kill her.'

Suddenly Godfrey noticed that Adoni wasn't in the room. 'Where's the boy?' he said.

Just then there was a movement outside, and Godfrey half swung me round. He pointed his gun into the darkness. 'Adoni!' I thought. 'And he's delivering the packet and himself to Manning!'

The next second I knew I was wrong. There was a sound of glass, of someone pouring out something, and then of singing.

'Hello, Manning,' said Sir Julian cheerfully. He had a glass of whisky in one hand and a bottle in the other. 'I hope you don't mind. I served myself. The bottle was on the terrace. I saw the light, so I came over . . . I thought Max might be here . . . Why, Lucy, my dear . . .'

He came forward, with a silly smile on his face, the smile of someone who had already drunk too much.

'Get into the room,' ordered Manning.

Sir Julian didn't seem to notice that there was anything wrong. I tried to speak and couldn't, and wondered why Max had said nothing. Then his father saw him. 'Why, Max . . .' he paused. 'The telephone's ringing,' he said. 'I wonder who it is. It can't be me because I'm here.'

'Get inside, you old fool!' said Godfrey, and he pulled on my arm.

Sir Julian smiled stupidly, raised the bottle – and then threw it, as hard as he could, at the light. He missed, but only just. The bottle caught the side of the lamp, which began to swing wildly, making it very difficult to see properly. I saw the white plaster of Spiro's broken leg. He stretched it out fast and caught Godfrey's legs.

Manning fired down and the plaster on the boy's leg flew into a thousand pieces. With a scream of pain, Spiro rolled over. Miranda threw herself on top of him.

I don't know how it happened, but suddenly I was free. As I fell, Manning fired again. Then something hit me violently, knocking me to the floor. It was Max throwing himself towards Godfrey's gun hand with murder in his eyes.

The two men fell out onto the terrace, fighting wildly. Papadopoulos ran out after them. Someone's arms closed round me, and held me tightly. Sir Julian! He smelt of whisky, but he certainly wasn't drunk. 'Are you all right, dear child?' he said.

I couldn't speak. I just held on to him, shaking.

The two men were still fighting like madmen on the terrace. Papadopoulos stood there with his gun ready to fire, but it was impossible to tell which man was Max and which

*Max threw himself towards Godfrey's gun hand with murder
in his eyes.*

was Godfrey. They were hanging over the side of the low terrace wall now, and Spiro pulled himself across the floor and raised his gun. Sir Julian pushed his hand down. 'No! Wait!' he said.

And then Max hit Godfrey in the face with great force and Godfrey fell back against the wall. For a second the two men were separated.

Spiro raised his gun and fired. The bullet hit the stone of the terrace wall, and Max, surprised, hesitated for a second. In that second Godfrey Manning rolled over the wall and dropped down into the bushes below. There was a crashing sound as he threw himself downhill and jumped down onto the path.

I rushed to Max, who was lying half over the edge of the terrace wall. 'Are you hurt?' I asked.

'No.' But he was already running down the steps from the terrace. We could see Godfrey below, as he thundered down the path – and also Adoni, now coming up from the boat-house with my packet. Adoni saw Godfrey, but he didn't try to stop him. He stepped back and hid behind the trees and Godfrey ran past him.

Miranda cried out, and Papadopoulos said with disbelief, 'He let him go!'

'He had to keep the proof safe,' I said quickly.

'He's a coward!' cried Miranda, and she ran to the steps. Max had stopped when he saw Adoni, but now he started to run after Godfrey again. Miranda ran past him, straight up to Adoni, and began to beat him with her hands. 'Coward! Coward! Coward!' she screamed. 'You let him go! If I were a man, I would eat his heart out!'

Adoni pushed her away, and he put his arm out to stop

Max. 'No, Max,' he said quietly. 'Wait. Wait and see.'

Suddenly the night was quiet. There was no wind now, and we heard the door of the boat-house close. Then there was the sound of Godfrey running to climb onto the boat. The engine started, and the boat left the boat-house, moving fast towards the open sea, and freedom.

And then the sound of the engine was drowned by a great noise as the boat exploded in a huge sheet of flame. The echo ran up the cliff, and rang out from rock to rock, until it died away, and only the sound of the trees was heard.

Sir Julian was saying, 'What happened? What happened?' and I heard a flood of Greek from Spiro. Papadopoulos was on the telephone, but he dropped it and ran out onto the terrace. 'Max! What's happened?' he cried.

With great difficulty, Max turned his eyes away from Adoni.

I said shakily. 'Er . . . when I was on the boat, I noticed that there was a smell of gas . . . It's very easy to leave a gas tap in the kitchen turned on . . . and very dangerous . . .'

'My God, what a night,' said the Inspector. 'Yes, I suppose it must have been the gas.'

'Did you get the packet, Adoni? I asked.

'Yes,' he replied.

'You've got a packet?' said the Inspector sharply. 'What's in it? A radio?'

'No,' I answered for Adoni. 'It's forged Albanian money. I stole it from Manning's boat and hid it in the boat-house before Manning took me out with him. I told Adoni where it was, and he went to fetch it.' I went on slowly, 'I think you'll find that this . . . accident . . . has prevented a lot of trouble. If the Greeks had had to shoot Manning . . .'

'You may be right, Miss Waring,' Papadopoulos replied. Then he turned to Petros. 'Are you all right? Come on, then. Let's go down.' And the two policemen went down the path towards the beach.

Everyone turned and looked at Adoni. He met our eyes, and smiled. He looked very beautiful. Miranda whispered, 'It was you . . . It was you . . .' and her face was shining with love. Adoni looked down at her, and said something very lovingly to her in Greek. And Max came to me, took me in his arms, and kissed me.

Sir Julian was waiting for us on the terrace. He was very pleased with his acting.

'Did you know he wasn't drunk?' I asked Max.

'Yes, but I didn't know what he was going to do. But what about you? How do you feel?'

'I'm all right,' I replied. I went over to the edge of the terrace and stared out to sea.

'Try to forget it now,' said Max, putting his arm round me.

Adoni and Miranda came softly up the terrace steps, heads bent, whispering, and went in through the french windows.

'What did Adoni say to Miranda, down there on the path?' I asked Max.

Max gave me a quick look, hesitated, then answered, 'He said "You wanted to eat his heart, my love. I have cooked it for you".'

'Dear God!' I said.

Sir Julian smiled. 'My poor child. You've seen the other face of this magical island tonight, haven't you? A very rough kind of magic for us – a musician, an actor, and an actress.'

'Oh, I don't think you can really call me an actress,' I protested.

'Then what about being a musician's wife?' asked Max.

'Do you think you could?' said Sir Julian. 'It would make me very happy.'

'I'm not sure which of you is asking me,' I laughed. 'But the answer to both of you is "Yes".'

Exercises

A Checking your understanding

Chapters 1–4 *Are these sentences true (T) or false (F)?*

1 Lucy was a very successful actress.
2 Miranda did not know if her father was alive or dead.
3 Lucy accused Max Gale of shooting at the dolphin.
4 Spiro couldn't swim.
5 Adoni would not marry Miranda without a dowry.
6 Sir Julian said that Lucy must pay a forfeit for the roses.

Chapters 5–8 *Find answers to these questions in the text.*

1 Who was the first person to join Lucy on the beach when she found the body?
2 Why was Lucy suspicious about Max Gale?
3 Why did Lucy go down to the beach in the middle of the night?
4 Why was it important to get the dolphin back into the sea quickly?
5 Why didn't Lucy want to tell Max about the dolphin?
6 How did they get the dolphin back into the sea?

Chapters 9–12 *Who in the story . . .*

1 . . . had a contact in Albania called Milo?
2 . . . wanted Sir Julian to find out what had happened to Spiro?
3 . . . brought Spiro home from Albania?
4 . . . telephoned Spiro's mother to tell her that Spiro was going out on the boat that night?
5 . . . took Spiro to Athens?
6 . . . found the proof in the cave?

Chapters 13–16 *Write answers to these questions.*

1 How did Lucy get into the boat-house?
2 Where did she hide the packet from the cave?
3 Why did Lucy come out of her hiding-place on the boat?
4 Why do you think Godfrey told Lucy about the forged Albanian money?
5 How did Lucy get back to the Castello dei Fiori?
6 Why did Lucy send Adoni down to the boat-house?
7 Why did Godfrey Manning's boat explode?

B Working with language

1 *Put this summary in the right order, and then join the parts together to make four sentences.*

1 For a while Max was afraid
2 and at first could not answer any questions sensibly.
3 When Max and Lucy returned to the Castello
4 that his father had said something about Spiro's rescue,
5 they found that Sir Julian had unexpectedly returned home.
6 but in fact Sir Julian had not told Manning anything.
7 who had given Sir Julian a lift home.
8 after rescuing the dolphin,
9 He was very drunk
10 Later, Max realized that it must have been Godfrey Manning

2 *Combine the short sentences in this passage into longer sentences, using linking words and making any other necessary changes.*

Godfrey found Lucy on his boat. Lucy pretended that she didn't know anything about Godfrey's secrets. Godfrey did not believe Lucy. Lucy realized that Godfrey was going to kill her. Lucy hit Godfrey and fought hard. Godfrey pulled out his gun. Lucy jumped over the side of the boat into the sea. The sea carried her towards the shores of Corfu. It was too far. Lucy began to drown. The dolphin came. The dolphin pushed Lucy towards the shore. A big wave rolled Lucy up the beach. Lucy fell unconscious on the sand.

C Activities

1 Max has just returned to the Castello after meeting Lucy for the first time, when she accuses him of shooting at the dolphin. Imagine the conversation Max has with his father, and write it down.

2 Write a description of one of the people in the story.

3 Imagine you are the Police Inspector. Write a short, official report for the newspapers, and give an innocent explanation for all the events, including the 'accident' that killed Godfrey Manning.

4 Write a paragraph about the island of Corfu for a holiday brochure.

Glossary

alcoholic (*n*) a person who drinks too much alcohol (e.g. whisky, beer)

bay (*n*) an area of sea enclosed by land on three sides

boom (*n*) a long piece of wood to keep the bottom of a sail stretched

bush a low thickly-growing plant, like a small tree

cabin a room on a boat

communist a person who believes that there should be no private ownership and that everything belongs to the state

coward a person who is not brave, who runs away from danger

deck the floor on a boat

dolphin an animal about two metres long that looks like a large fish and lives in the sea

dowry money or property brought by a wife to her husband on marriage

dressing-gown a coat that is worn in the house over nightclothes

drift (*v*) to be carried along by wind or water

drunk (*adj*) excited or confused by too much alcoholic drink

Empress the female Head of a country, like a Queen

flare (*n*) a flame or torch which is lit when a boat is in trouble

footstep the sound or mark of a step when someone is walking

forfeit (*n*) a kind of punishment for doing something wrong or losing in a game

forge (*v*) to make a copy or imitation of something (e.g. money) in order to deceive people

french windows windows that are also doors (opening into a garden)

gin a strong, colourless alcoholic drink

godfather a man who promises, when a child is baptized, to be responsible for its well-being

great-grandfather the grandfather of your mother or father

magic the power to do wonderful or extraordinary things that cannot be explained scientifically

magical so delightful or wonderful that it seems unreal

mainland the main part of a country, not the islands around it

nervous breakdown an illness of the mind caused by worry and problems

plaster (*n*) a hard white case put round a broken leg or arm to hold the broken bone in place until it mends

play (*n*) a story acted in a theatre or on television, etc.

procession a long line of people or cars moving along slowly

propeller pieces of metal that spin round to drive a ship or aeroplane

purr (*v*) to make the sound a cat makes when it is happy

rail (*n*) a horizontal piece of wood or metal fixed as a hand-hold

rock (*v*) to move backwards and forwards, or from side to side

saint a very good, holy person, believed by the church to have a special place in heaven after death

shade (*n* and *v*) a place sheltered from sunlight or bright light

shark a large sea-fish which can attack and kill people

slip (*v*) to slide accidentally and fall down

smuggle (*v*) to take things secretly in or out of a country without paying the necessary taxes

stern (*n*) the back end of a boat

stowaway (*n*) a person who hides on a boat in order to travel without paying or being seen

swing (*n*) to turn or move suddenly from one side to another

switch (*v*) to connect or disconnect the power to a light, machine, etc.

surface (*v*) to come up into the air from under the water

tame (*v*) to teach an animal not to be afraid of people

tape (*n*) a thin metallic ribbon used for recording music

tempest a storm (*The Tempest* is a play by William Shakespeare)

terrace a level, paved area beside a house where people can sit, eat, etc. outdoors

tight fixed or held in a very firm or strong way

tiller the long piece of wood that controls the steering of a small boat

trail (*n*) marks or signs in a long line left by something passing by

traitor someone who does something disloyal to his country, a friend, a belief, etc.

twins a pair of children born of the same mother at the same time

value (*n*) how much something is worth

villa a house, often a holiday house by the seaside or in the countryside